Gentle Spirits

Thomas Ford Conlan

Legacy Book Press LLC
Camanche, Iowa

For my grandsons: Grady, Zeke, and Walker.

"*A ship is safe in the harbor, but that is not why ships are built.*"

—Variation of a quote attributed to Albert Einstein and others.

Acknowlegements

I wish to thank early readers of *Gentle Spirits*, particularly Betty Henne for her thoughtful complete edit of the first draft; and my old pal, Michael Brantley, who provides constant, positive feedback for my work. Poet Ellen Lord and writer Edd Tury offered insightful comments as Beta readers.

Fellow writers Shuly X. Cawood, Annie Fitzmaurice, John Wemlinger, and John "Yoni" Levin helped me see the light in preparing the synopsis.

I cannot forget Jodie Toohey of Legacy Book Press who saw the value in *Gentle Spirits*. Often work is overlooked by publishers and agents. I am grateful to Jodie for taking the time to read and publish my work.

The characters in *Gentle Spirits* are fictional, yet most writers and readers know that fiction stems from reality. I feel fortunate for my many friends, both here and gone, whose traits contributed to the characters in the book.

I am a lucky man to have such a loving and supporting family. My wife, Artist Glenda Catherine Conlan, sat through many morning readingsto help me to develop the final version. My forebears, my father, grandfather, my son James, daughters Elsa and Katy, daughter-in-law Monica, and sons-in-law Josh and Sean, all appear in some form and some way as *Gentle Spirits*.

Gentle Spirits is a generational saga, giving meaning to the past and hope for the future of my grandsons, Grady, Zeke, and Walker.

Contents

CHAPTER ONE:
SAMUEL FIRESTONE THOMPSON
1950-1955

Samuel

He was born under the sign of fire, on a day in deep December when lake effect snow blew flakes as large as pancakes. His dying mother stared out through prisms created by drops melted on the windows of their cabin in the north woods. As an avid reader of the Bible, she favored the name Samuel, not that she was overly religious, but she liked the stories.

As life drained from her delicate frame, she called her husband, Firestone Thompson, to the chair where she lay covered by a hand-sewn quilt. Her grandmother had created patterns of multiple crossed ovals that even now reminded her of the symbol for infinity.

The man held his son close. She dabbed her fingers into a cast iron pot that simmered on the woodstove to add moisture to the dry heat of the fire. She spread drops of warm water over the baby's head, and with her last words, spoke his name.

"Samuel … Firestone … Thompson …"

The sun broke from the clouds and the snow stopped. A bright red cardinal flew into a green cedar outside the window. The female, duller but still tinged with red, broke free of the nest, fluttered through the cedar boughs, and swooped away into the nearby woods.

Firestone raised Samuel up to the window. A large doe appeared out of the trees, walked to the bird feeder, and nibbled on sunflower seeds that had fallen to the ground. She grew skittish, sensing a presence, and bounded away back to cover. Moments later, a bothered, ten-point buck rushed out of the woods and skidded to a stop. He dipped his high, pointed rack to the earth and sniffed momentarily where the doe had marked the snow, and in a late-season rut, charged wildly in pursuit across a partially frozen creek.

Firestone vowed to never speak of his wife again.

THE FIRST WINTERS

Firestone and his infant son grew together during that first winter in the woods. The elements acted as a constant reminder that they were truly alone. The father planned his necessary chores around the baby's sleep. He had put up enough firewood to last until spring. He parboiled corn and green beans from the garden and mixed in a bit of butter before packing the vegetables in the old chest freezer. Red skin potatoes were covered and kept cool in the fieldstone cellar, along with a few dozen bottles of sweet wine they had brewed together, before she had become frail.

He had so enjoyed the time in September when the grapes sweetened on the vine, and the corn grew so tender, edible without cooking, fresh from the stalk. She had loved the time, too, he told himself. She had wanted to move to the woods. Money had not driven them north, away from people and into the wild. Firestone had banked away his profits over the years, and in addition to these thousand acres up north, he had the seaside cottage on St. Simons Island. He had promised to take her south in the spring.

Venison sausage and dried jerky hung alongside onions in the cellar, and when Samuel slept in the evening, Firestone could slip down to the creek for a brook trout to vary his own protein. They had packed away canned milk and formula, and wheat flour and Pablum from the Three-Corners General Store some twenty miles distant, packed enough to last until spring.

Damned if I'll make the trip to town now.

The ground hadn't frozen solid. He had wrapped her in a wool blanket patterned in Black Watch tartan plaid. Firestone formed a casket from hand-hewn cedar planks. He dug a hole deep, behind the garden, in a spot near the apple trees with a view of the rising sun over forested hills to the east. He gathered fieldstones in varied shapes and sizes, greenstone and granite, mica and flecks of red, and balanced the stones, largest on the bottom, into a cairn that grew like a miniature pyramid toward the sky. At Christmas, the lake effect snows had come and buried the cairn except for the top few stones where he gazed every morning from a window. After Samuel had been fed, Firestone sat by the wood fire with coffee and a book. A brown-tinged-yellow dog lay at his feet and kept a watchful eye on the sleeping boy child.

Firestone read and re-read Emerson's essays and the poems of Robert Frost. He thumbed through passages of his Grandmother's Holy Bible, the one with their family tree inked on the inside cover and comments scribbled in the margins. Over and over he marveled at the handwritten record of Dougal Dee Thompson, born in 1804 in Edinburgh, Scotland. He took pride in the spunk and spirit it must have taken to emigrate through the Canadian wilderness in the early nineteenth century and to build a successful life and family in the new world. Firestone felt that same spirit, deep in his soul. But Dougal Dee had a partner in his life of travel, a Miss Jane Cousins of London. Firestone's partner lay beneath a cairn covered in snow in the highland woods of Northern Michigan.

Winter days passed quickly while the nights never ended. Samuel was a good baby and slept once the shadows fell in late afternoon until the witching hours of early morning. Firestone set his wound chronometer at *zero-four-hundred hours* upon Samuel's twitching. He rolled out of bed and struck a match to light a flame on the propane stove. While the milk warmed, Firestone stoked the woodstove to Samuel's lyrical chanting. He tested the white liquid on his wrist before lifting his son into his arms and soothing the child's cries.

Samuel ate vigorously, and once satisfied, again rested soundly. During these lulls, Firestone often drifted back asleep in the rocker holding his child, until on sunny winter mornings, the chirps of birds outside on the feeder rousted him from slumber. The birds were demanding, even in the dead of winter. Firestone met their demands religiously and kept the feeders full of sunflower seeds he had dried from the garden in the fall. A pair of bright cardinals came each day, first the duller female, then the bright male. Chickadees and goldfinches flitted about tirelessly. Firestone held Samuel close to the window, and together they watched friends come and go unmolested by the muddy-colored barn cat who was unable to navigate the deep snow to bother the birds. Father and son waited for the spring thaw, waited for the robins, and waited for the bluebirds of late spring.

Patches of dirt began to appear by the middle of March. Samuel grew tired of a milk diet, and like the birds, demanded more. Firestone first mixed the Pablum, enough for both of them, as he too enjoyed the warm chunks of flour for breakfast. Soon enough, he began to mush up apples and potatoes and acorn squash, always preparing enough for himself.

On sunny days, Firestone wrapped the boy in a blanket and tucked him inside his leather knapsack so that only the child's face shown from beneath his covered head. Together they snowshoed through the woods and enjoyed the melting snow and the warm sun on their faces. Charlie, a loose mix of shepherd and lab, usually led the way, or romped side trails, and covered three times as much ground. Firestone recognized the tracks of deer who wintered in the valley and could differentiate between a buck's wide webbed hoofs and the marks of the coyote and wolves who chased the deer. He stopped to consider the blow holes in the deep snow the partridge made to breathe.

Ice had begun to break up on the creek that ran through the valley below the cabin. On a sunny afternoon, with the baby on his back, Firestone cast a lure on his lightweight rod, and spun the reel to make the lure swim through the clear water and attract a brook trout.

Could Samuel remember? "Aye," Firestone would say, and it was no wonder that Samuel's speech gained a touch of the Scots.

From his youngest days, Samuel knew how to handle a rod and reel. He had always known where to cast, beneath an overhanging cedar, or near a deep edge between dark and light. He had always known where trout lived.

Firestone didn't make the trip south to the Georgia barrier islands that first spring, nor the second or third. He taught Samuel the way of the woods, the changing seasons, and how to hunt and gather the morels that grew following the first warm rains in May. The first spring, Firestone planted the garden with Samuel on his back. By the second, Samuel wandered about in the fresh turned soil and wondered at the earthworms he held in tiny hands. In his third year, Samuel stuck corn kernels into soft dirt under his father's watchful eye. Together, they studied the daily change, how twin green leaves burst up in soldierly rows after ten days. They pruned the grapevines and cut the apple trees back to nubs. They needed and wanted for nothing, nothing except the touch of a woman.

The Ocean

A double-wide, clapboard boathouse stood near the high-water mark on the southwest coast of the island. Firestone had been gone from the saltwater for nearly ten years. During that time, he had lost the love of his life and begun to raise a son.

With young Samuel by his side, he cut the lock and pried open the man door to the shed. The young boy marveled at the size of a spider, who had spun a web nearly five feet in diameter across a window frame. Caulk peeled along the wooden munnions of the window. Humid and windless sea air filled the shadowed space. Firestone picked up a mallet and knocked a bolt free from the locking channel of the double swing doors. Sunlight flooded in.

Dust covered the sleek mahogany hull of a twenty-four-foot sailing sloop. The second craft, a twenty-one-foot, wood-strake Thompson runabout, was covered with a canvas tarp secured tight to an oak plank cradle. A pair of dolphins swam past some twenty yards out. One raised an eye toward shore while the other playfully flipped a tailfin.

"Aye, we have our work cut out for us," Firestone told his son, who stared in a trance at the powerful swimming mammals.

Firestone untied the tarps from the runabout, and with Samuel's help, folded them neatly and stored them in the rafters. He removed the blocks holding the cradle secure on the wooden railway.

"Stand aside, now."

With his strong shoulders against the wooden hull, Firestone shoved the Thompson runabout out the door and down the rails into sunlight. He rigged a water hose for Samuel and climbed aboard with liquid Ivory and a scrub brush. They covered every exposed inch of the boat. Father scrubbed while the son rinsed and occasionally raised the hose a bit too far to douse his father with cool spray. The dolphins circled closer as the tide continued to flood.

Firestone opened the engine hatch and changed the sparkplugs. He showed Samuel how to set the correct gap.

The boy might not understand now, but someday he will need to know, might save his life.

He walked the boat further down the rails so that the prop and cooling water intake were submerged. He lifted Samuel aboard and hoisted himself up. He turned the key, and the throaty Chrysler engine roared.

With Samuel on his lap, Firestone pulled back on the throttle and backed into the rising tide. Firestone turned the wheel seaward, out the buoyed channel. Dolphins rose and fell with the bow wake. A gentle, two-foot swell rolled in long periods.

Firestone placed his hand over Samuel's small fingers on the stick. The craft rose into a plane over the swells, and together they flew toward the red St. Simons sea buoy, and the blue ocean beyond.

Floating, Samuel remembered, from deep in his subconscious, floating.

Chapter Two:
Marie and Angelique
1948

WINDWARD ISLANDS

Angelique tanned easily. She never burned. Her mother had passed along pigments of light brown skin that seemed to override her father's ruddy complexion. Angelique reveled in the sun. From her father, she received emerald eyes that turned azure in varying light the way the sea surrounding her home island of Martinique changed color and tone when clouds rolled by.

Collon had emigrated from County Antrim near the North Sea before World War II broke out. He sailed a wooden ketch that carried wealthy vacationers on once in a lifetime trips, south to St. Lucia and Grenada in the Leeward Islands, even as far as Belize if the money was right. Or perhaps he'd take the forty-five-foot vessel north to Saint Martin and across the straits to his favorite anchorage in British Anguilla before making a hazardous overnight trip to the Virgin Islands.

Before Angelique, Marie sailed along with Collon to cook fresh-caught tuna on the fantail grill and to keep sultry, young women away. Temptation ran swiftly along with the currents in the southern latitudes, where late on a balmy night, the Southern Cross rose above the equator.

After Angelique, Marie stayed on the island to care for the child. She would hold Angelique and watch Collon's comings and goings from a distant perch on a hillock above the bay.

Marie stared as the ketch sailed out of the St. Martin channel, crossed the barrier reef, and turned west toward the Virgins. Bothered by an argument the night before, when Marie had urged Collon to postpone the trip, she somehow knew this night crossing with four souls aboard might be Collon's last voyage.

A too formal British officer at the consulate in Tortola told Marie not to visit the bullet-riddled, half-sunk ketch. She had packed their few belongings in a duffel, and with baby Angelique on her hip, caught the ferry to the British Virgins.

"Pirates," he said, "nothing left on board. Blood suggests the men were killed and tossed overboard. They left no sign of the two young women. I suspect they were violated and taken to be sold in the sex trade. Quite a common occurrence, actually. Did you know the passengers?"

Marie ran from the stone building toward the holding dock. She carefully wrapped a blanket around her baby and set her down on the green grass growing in a park near the shore end of the pier. As she jumped aboard Collon's boat, the ketch rolled with her weight. She spread her legs to balance on the wooden deck to wait for the recovery roll, and realizing that the boat would not regain equilibrium, worked her way to the wheel. Marie noticed spots of blood as she reached down and removed a hidden, loose section of the deck board to reveal a drawer-like compartment.

The British officer hurried down the dock and called to her, "Off the boat now missus, off the boat, now."

Furtively, yet with purpose, Marie spied the roll of cash she knew Collon had hidden there. She stuck the wad beneath her white sun dress in her panty bottoms. She reached to cover the compartment and noticed a reflection from a shiny black object, Collon's prized shark's tooth. She slipped the rawhide necklace around her head and returned the loose deck board cover just before the officer rounded the sail. "What are you doing there, missus? Come off there now, no need to see that."

THE STATES

The cash roll proved substantial. Marie peeled off the first layer like the brown paper skin of an onion.

So much cash. Where had Collon made so much money? Well, no matter now. Enough to take care of Angelique properly.

She needed papers and a passport good in the U.S. Marie had always wanted to see the States, to see the places the swells spoke of so easily. She would go to the west, maybe meet up with a cowboy, or go to the north woods. Marie wondered at the thought of trees. She would stay away from the cities, the northeast coast of the States; too much pavement, too many people.

Marie liked the barely broken silence of a quiet morning when she struggled to identify bird calls. She heard a new call the morning Collon had left while she rocked baby Angelique on the front porch of their rented cabana. She asked aloud while looking into her Angel's eyes, "What kind of bird makes that sound? No doubt a colorful bird, to sound so sweet."

The Naval officer asked Marie to return the following day to settle affairs. As she walked down the steps of the Crown building, she noticed the ketch straining on taut lines and falling deeper into the slip. With a leather knapsack containing all that she owned slung over one shoulder and Angelique held tightly with her other arm, she hurried into the busy marketplace and became lost in the crowd.

Marie found an out of the way table under a wooden arbor. Frangipani vines drooped downward toward her. The sweet, scented cascade hid her from passing foot traffic. She needed a boost and something to calm her nerves, so when the waiter, a native islander in a starched white shirt came by, she ordered Pusser's and cola with a twist of fresh lime "and coconut milk for Angelique, s'il vous plait."

Locals with pan-formed steel drums rang a beat from a dusty lot across the street. She knew she would miss the freedom of the islands, but a voice inside told her it was time to leave. A bluebird perched on the tip of a sundial in the café's courtyard. She heard the gentle song above the noise of the market, between beats on a tin pan.

The waiter returned, "Another?"

"Non, just the one, merci."

"A boat then? Perhaps you are looking for passage?"

Landfall

During the night she heard a deep metallic tone. A bell? Marie felt Angelique's warm breath on her neck and carefully adjusted her position on the canvas bunk to keep from awakening the sleeping child. She wanted to roll over, to return to the dream, but the bell nagged at her.

In the dark compartment, she raised her head to the glass portlight. A deep mist covered the water. Light emanated from a dull-edged, formless moon, reminding her of a white-clothed damsel floating above the sea.

Marie heard movement on the deck above and then the low rumble of the sailboat's diesel motor turning over.

A bell buoy, landfall, we have come to America.

She dressed Angelique, wrapped the infant in a blanket, and placed her in a sling that fit over her head and one shoulder but allowed free movement of her hands. She picked up the knapsack and climbed the ladder up into the cockpit.

"I'll take the other half now," the grisly, unshaven captain whispered.

"When my Angelique is safe, sur la shore."

The Captain sneered and turned to guide the boat toward a barrier island becoming visible in the distance. He directed the young Bahamian deckhand to the bow with a boathook. He eased off the throttle. The craft drifted toward a sand bar several yards off a beach where large four-legged shapes appeared curious. "Wild ponies," the boy said. "Cumberland Island, no one will question you here."

The boat scratched against a sandy bottom, and while the Captain was intent upon a controlled backing down of the craft, she reached into a hidden pocket and handed him five one-hundred-dollar bills American, and made her way forward to the bow.

The boy took her free hand and held her weight while she lowered herself into the cool, briny, waist-deep saltwater. When the Captain turned his head, she slipped the boy a colorful Bahamian note, and he gently eased his grip, "Careful now, Mum, you and the little one."

Marie waded ashore.

The lead pony stomped a hoof on the sand.

The boat backed away quickly and disappeared into the mist.

Cumberland Island

Marie heard the deep rumble of a large marine diesel motor and hurried to hide further ashore behind a stand of live oak. The ponies heard the noise too and broke into a trot down the beach away from the intruder. As the sun burned the dawn mist, she watched a coastal patrol boat round the southern point of the island.

She had heard the stories about postwar Georgia. Marie knew that she could not pass off her olive-brown skin as a tan, not among these bone-white natives, though her beauty was flawless. Her fetching lines had always brought her trouble from men, even from Collon, though she never regretted Angelique. Her Angelique, lighter yet, and with her father's Irish blood, she might pass.

The patrol boat continued up the coast without changing course. The yearling child twisted against Marie's bosom and opened her eyes slowly, her cheeks indented where she had rested upon a button. Sitting in the sandy grass beneath a spreading live oak, Marie lifted the child, and with her strong hands beneath Angelique's shoulders, held her high in the air. The child smiled down on the mother, seeming to revel in the moment.

Marie offered Angelique her breast and the child suckled while the mother took a deep breath and sighed. After a time, Marie helped Angelique to her wobbly bare feet and held tightly to her hands while she attempted to walk in the sand. Angelique stumbled, landing softly. Marie lifted Angelique again and again. A few of the ponies returned and looked on curiously as the child learned to walk.

Marie gathered their sparse belongings into the knapsack and felt for the hidden money roll in an inside pocket several times. She lifted Angelique to her hip and walked with purpose toward a column of smoke she had seen billowing from the leeward side of the island.

She came upon a grand white mansion with manicured lawns. A dark-skinned servant scurried around the far corner of the house. She worked her way around to the rear where she found the older gentleman, greying at his temples, who led a horse-drawn cart full of firewood toward the kitchen.

"What ya got there, Mis'? Aw, a pretty little thing. Where y'all goin'? Tell Hector, now."

Angelique smiled, and somehow Marie felt she could trust this old soul. "Je voudrais, travail, ah, work," she replied, struggling to find the English for her words.

"If you can cook, I'll take you to see Missus' Camille. We been needing a cook since Lucinda passed on to the heavenly place."

The grand lady Camille took to Marie right away, perhaps because of Angelique's stunning beauty, or perhaps because the spring high season had arrived and she needed a cook for her party guests.

She led Marie to a small room off the kitchen, "Hector will show you your duties once you've cleaned up. I hope the baby won't be a problem."

Hector found a baby bed in the attic, and while Marie and the child bathed in fresh, warm water for the first time in weeks, he set an old steel-spring double bed in a corner of the small room off the kitchen and beat the dust from a thin, down-filled mattress. He got a fire going in the behemoth, white porcelain cook stove, and when Marie had dressed and put Angelique down for a nap, he gave her a cursory tour of the kitchen.

The wooden screen door slammed as Hector left with a wave, "Midday dinner Mis' Marie, they'll be eight of dem', and don' forget Hector, I'll be working up an appetite."

Marie stood at the sink and gazed out through a twelve-paneled window. An island deer with antlers shaped in a large vee munched on early wild alfalfa growing across a wetland estuary. In the foreground, she saw an unkempt spice garden with weeds beginning to overtake young green leaves of rosemary, sage, and the first sprouts of mint.

Three iceboxes stood like soldiers at attention on an opposite wall. She opened each in turn. One held fresh beef, venison, and lamb, some hand-dressed poultry, and other game birds. Another contained fresh milk, eggs, and cream stored amongst cheeses in myriad shapes wrapped in cloth. In the last, kept cool but not cold, she found fresh vegetables.

Marie chose three pullets and washed them in cold water. She chopped up two loaves of day-old bread along with sweet onions from the pantry. From the garden, she picked fresh sage and early shallots and mixed them lightly with an egg in a large ceramic bowl before stuffing the birds. She checked the temperature in the first oven with a thermometer attached to a rack, and when it read three hundred seventy degrees, placed the chickens in the oven.

Marie went about her tasks with a light heart on this bright morning where the sun was cut only by the Spanish moss that hung like ghosts from the live oaks in the yard. In the other oven, she baked sweet potatoes for pie, and on the burner above, boiled white potatoes to mash. She chopped and squared a cantaloupe and a light green melon.

Angelique breathed easily in her sleep, no doubt relaxed by the savory smells wafting through the kitchen to her bed. The same warm smells must have worked their way up the narrow staircase to the formal dining room. Marie heard Camille's footsteps on the wooden planks. The folks upstairs were anxious to eat.

Marie called to Hector who had also been drawn to the screen door, "M 'aider, help, please?"

She asked Hector to finish loading the dishes into the dumb waiter, washed her hands, checked her hair in a mirror, and climbed the stairway to a new life.

Chapter Three:
Sally and Firestone
1941-1950

WANDERLUST

The train out of Chicago bound to Rapid City lurched along like a team of draft horses. Tracks built upon loose gravel had been known to give way, and the engineer was easy on the throttle despite the half-empty rot-gut whiskey bottle propped between his legs.

Firestone dug the heavy, wooden handled shovel into the coal bin. He lifted a load and tossed the fresh, black Pennsylvania rock into a glowing burner. A blast of heat fought back at him. He cursed the furnace while swinging the iron door closed. He cursed the lazy, half-drunk engineer who couldn't hear a word above the din. Firestone hung his head out the back window. Wind cooled the sweat from his face.

The reality of leaving home seemed much harder than the dream. With the confidence of a young man, Firestone left the safety of his uncle's farm in his wake. The Thompson family land had been passed down through three generations since the patriarch Dougal Dee Thompson emigrated from Scotland in 1844. Dougal Dee wed a Miss Elizabeth Jane Cousins from Dorset, England, some twenty years his younger, before setting out for the New World. The couple worked their way from Liverpool, across the Atlantic Ocean, and up the Saint Lawrence River. They settled for a time in Woodstock, Ontario, as Miss Jane had become with child.

With his young family, Dougal Dee continued his trek westward to St. Clair County, Michigan, where land was available to those who knew how to work. He settled several sections along the Black River, before the call to end slavery rang over his new land.

A staunch believer in freedom for all mankind, Dougal Dee volunteered for the 4th Michigan Cavalry. A gallant horseman, he rose to the rank of Captain, serving under General Ulysses Sam Grant in the fight to control the Mississippi River. The "4th" was instrumental in the capture of Jefferson Davis, thwarting his efforts to flee retribution for crimes against humanity.

Dougal Dee's son and Firestone's Grandfather, Arnold Ellsworth Thompson, followed the family tradition atop a horse under Teddy Roosevelt, as the Rough Riders took San Juan Hill in Cuba and forced a treaty with Spain. Arnold returned from the Spanish-American War to marry and resume a pastoral life on the family farm.

Firestone's father, John Milton Thompson, grew up on the farm, but never took to life working the earth. He left for college in Detroit, married spritely Maggie Newberry, and built a successful accounting career in the burgeoning auto industry. When World War I broke out, the industry turned from building automobiles to manufacturing the implements of modern conflict. John Milton had not served in the Army but had been a vital cog in the supply of armaments to the U.S. forces in Europe fighting the Kaiser.

John Milton's younger brother, Douglas, returned from the *War to End All Wars* a changed man. He relished the restorative peace of farming alongside his father, while Mother Ada tended the dairy cows, and always had dinner waiting at noon, and supper at five. Days in sunny fields aboard the John Deere diesel provided an outlet for memories Douglas never spoke aloud.

Arnold passed the original farm in a partnership to John Milton and Douglas. By the time Firestone came along, his Uncle Douglas had expanded the holdings, adding over 600 acres of rich, black dirt. Firestone's mother, Maggie, died from the cancer at thirty-four when Firestone was still a youngster. John Milton took the young lad to live with his Grandmother Ada. She taught him to read and write and think, but Firestone learned his love of the land from his Grandfather.

Young Firestone had a burning urge to travel and see the world. Something was missing in his life, a duty unfulfilled. In June of 1941, he left the safety of Michigan to explore the west. The Winchester Model 1894 had been a parting gift from his Uncle Douglas, an unspoken message.

The right to live free on the land must be earned.

A herd of antelope appeared from behind mounds in the seemingly flat prairie before disappearing behind the optical illusion of rolling grasslands. While looking ahead into the breeze, Firestone spotted a lone, lingering buck browsing in the stubble that grew near the base of a ridge. The engineer also noticed the deer and eased back on the throttle to slow the train without engaging the brakes.

Firestone lifted his Winchester Model 1894 from a rack above the window and cocked the lever. A shell slid into the chamber. Firestone rested his left arm on the sill, adjusted his aim at an appropriate height, and waited for the mule deer to enter the open sight. With a young man's reflexes, Firestone felt the train slow, and without hesitation, timed a shot perfectly into the animal's heart.

The engineer applied the brakes, and the train screeched to a hard stop. Firestone jumped down and strode toward his kill. He placed his left hand on the mulie's still-warm shoulder. While passengers stared from the train's windows, he turned toward the Black Hills that loomed in the distance. He closed his eyes for a moment, as his great-grandfather, Dougal Dee Thompson, had taught each of the men in his line.

A silent prayer of thanks to heaven and the great unknown.

The cook's helper arrived and field-dressed the buck with a sharp bowie-knife. He then lifted the animal across his shoulders and hauled the carcass to a boxcar. He strung the meat up to hang, pulled the fresh hide down and off, stretched the fur out on the wooden boxcar floor, and spread coarse salt on the skin to dry. The meat would cure for a few days, and the crew would enjoy venison steaks on the return run from Rapid City.

When the train reached Rapid, Firestone asked the conductor for his pay and disembarked with nary a word to the foul engineer. He strung his leather knapsack over his shoulder. In one hand, he held his Winchester. In the other, he fingered a smooth bone antler. He figured to find a tempered-steel blade up in the mining town of Lead and form himself a knife.

Buffalo

Firestone hiked up a steep hill, reaching a clapboard shack that housed the headquarters of the Lead Gold Mining Company. The clatter of rail cars hauling ore up from below bounced off canyon walls and echoed as he pushed open the door. He met the eyes of a tall and rangy man who looked to be in charge.

"Looking for work," he offered. "My name is Firestone Thompson."

"John Macmaster," the man replied, looking Firestone up and down as if to gauge the young man. "I'm the foreman of this hell hole, the men call me Mac. Any experience running machinery?"

"I was raised on a farm. Drove our John Deere Diesel tractor when I turned twelve."

Mac walked Firestone to the bunkhouse. "The name of the town and the mine is *'leed,'* for a lead of gold in the rock, not *'led,'* like the mineral. Stow your gear here, take any open bunk. I'll keep the Winchester locked in my office for now."

Huge rock shards blasted from the canyon face piled like rubble at the base. Firestone quickly learned his job: to ease the tracked steam shovel close enough to lift a load of ore, reverse his track, pivot, and dump the load into a rock crusher. He fell into a seemingly mindless job that required acute concentration and manual dexterity. Day after day he watched as the crushed ore flushed out and filled bucket-like rail cars that clanked up the steep slope to the refinery building. Gold ran through the rock, but Firestone seldom saw any shine.

The days lasted long but the camp cook knew how to keep the crew happy. Firestone spent any free daylight hours walking the hills and exploring. He desperately wanted to see a buffalo herd. An old Lakota the men called Jim, though that wasn't his name, worked a hand shovel and bunked next to Firestone. Jim talked of trout filling the streams and game aplenty in the *Paha Sapa*, the land stolen from his people for the gold he now seeked. Firestone fell into the daily routine of the mine and treasured his time after dark to study the history of the Black Hills region. Firestone began to understand.

Land cannot be owned forever.

Late on a Saturday afternoon, just before the whistle, the crew was in a yank to hit the bars uptown. A tow-headed kid, barely out of school forgot to set the brake on a railcar full of slag. The iron cart began to roll, picked up speed on the steep hill, and jumped the tracks. The car flipped twice before coming to an abrupt halt against a concrete trestle where Old Jim, head down, had been shoveling debris from the tracks. The stray iron cart pinned Jim's now limp body against the abutment.

Firestone helped carry old Jim to a wagon and rode along to the undertaker in town. "Unclaimed," the man in black commented, "most of these Indians go unclaimed."

Firestone had earned his stake. He returned to the mine office. "Mac, I'll be moving on. I'll take my pay that's due in gold coin, and my Winchester."

On his way out of town, Firestone dropped a gold coin off with the undertaker, "Take proper care of this man."

He set out to explore the Black Hills, where an old Lakota had told him, "Trout run like water droplets in a shower down Spearfish Creek."

Firestone woke chilled from dew that covered the mountain-forest floor. His campfire had dwindled to one, barely glowing coal. Birds whistled, hidden in a canopy of green. He whistled back and waited. Soon a faceless chorus echoed from the woods.

He had camped on a grass plateau surrounded by boulders, far removed from occasional vacationers with silver trailers shaped like torpedoes. He dreaded fireworks and kids with sparklers and found an isolated campsite. Shadows from his illegal fire danced against the boulders and provided all the company he needed.

The outline of a buffalo appeared above the fire in the night sky.

Firestone rolled over in his blanket and slept soundly. In the morning, he rose and walked to the edge of the plateau. He found himself on a ridge overlooking a herd of monolithic shapes spotting the hillside. Buffalo grazed below.

He packed his gear and hiked, following a wide, green valley formed over eons by a small creek. He had started just after dawn, so walked unbothered by the noise of civilization that certainly would grow with the day. He seeked the wild and unfettered.

A killdeer feigned a broken wing and hopped purposefully over the broken ground of the Dakota high desert. Firestone took the cue and turned north to avoid upsetting the bird protecting her nest. He stopped and looked back several times to wonder at the Black Hills rising from the flatland and understood how the range had been named. But in his effort to avoid the nest, his eyes were drawn to a solitary shape growing out of the prairie some ten miles distant.

He changed course without pause.

Firestone hiked with a vengeance toward the lone butte. He let himself be drawn in, as if he were on a tether. He let his mind go and his will subside. The ground rose. He watched as each step of his boots kicked up dust.

In the warm sun, he learned how the prairie can deceive the eye; how the seemingly flat horizon gives way to a draw that drops into a wallow; how the brown, dying grass gives way to lush green in a creek valley. He wondered at the source of a trickling creek in such dry country.

A mule deer jumped, startled by his presence. Firestone marveled at the girth of the buck, much heavier than white tail deer back home, and the antler rack, so wide, so very thick. He rubbed his fingers on the smooth, bone handle of his knife.

Firestone reached the mysterious butte just as the sun began to set. He made camp in the flowing grassland at the southern base. A nearly full moon shown white in the evening sky over the outline of a lone, majestic mountain.

I will camp here tonight, and in the morning, hike to the top.

FIRESTONE CLIMBS THE GOOD MOUNTAIN

Firestone woke with a yearning. The new day held a promise that he could not quite identify. He skipped breakfast and stowed his gear under a basswood tree that grew overhanging a trickling creek. Moving up a broad and gentle slope through high grasses tinged golden with the sun, he stepped carefully to avoid crushing tiny yellow and purple wildflowers that dotted the landscape.

Far above, a solitary peak loomed in holy contrast to the dust of civilization kicking up some twenty miles away in the Sturgis valley. A few buffalo grazed in the prairie grasses. He crossed an iron cattle grate where a gravel road met fences on either side and walked past a wooden sign etched,

Entering the Bear Butte Cheyenne Reservation.

The road continued up a gentle slope to a plateau where a wooden A-frame house apparently served as the caretaker's residence. A walk-out basement faced west and opened out to a windowed vista of dry prairie cut in the distance by the meandering green of the Belle Fourche River.

A middle-aged Cheyenne man sat outside on a rock retaining wall smoking a hand-rolled cigarette. His deep, olive eyes emanated calm. His long flowing ponytail showed traces of grey that accented his pure black hair.

The native man asked Firestone softly, "Where is your homeland?"

He responded, "Michigan, Chippewa country."

The man grinned and answered, "My wife's brother lives in Michigan, up near Peshawbetown."

The man's friendly manner put Firestone at ease as he listened. "Our traditions, and our sacred beliefs, passed down through generations by spoken word, shroud *Noavosse* in mystery. Some folks say that Bear Butte was formed by a volcano that never erupted. Enjoy your sacred walk."

Firestone felt the growing power of molten lava captured within the depths of the earth under this seemingly calm mountain-cap of solid rock. He reasoned how, similarly, man's explosive nature hides beneath a blanket he creates for himself. Firestone fought his own demons of eruption, a youthful temper that comes in flame and fury and leaves like a scolded dog dragging his tail between his legs.

He knew he needed to let go of anger and resentment. He wanted to sit in sunlight on the peak of this good mountain, to transcend the burdensome ties of time, and if only for a moment, find strength and patience from the power of the earth. Firestone felt a surge of energy rise through his diaphragm, spread into his arms, and tingle his senses.

A force drove each step, ever upward. His mind began to challenge long held assumptions. He passed through bright colors, and upon close inspection, discovered the colors were ragged bits of torn clothing tied to scraggly tree branches. Holy rags, like candles in a chapel, had been left in remembrance, in hope, or in honor, of loved ones. He climbed slowly, as if through a graveyard of spirits, one step at a time, and breathed in a fresh essence. Exertion cleared his mind, and gradually, the mountain absorbed him.

If you listen, the mountain will answer.

He looked upward to a split, where the singular path separated into two distinct routes. A simple choice awaited. A steep, more aggressive path, certainly a quicker route, came fraught with potential danger. Several hundred yards further up and ahead, he saw the diverted paths rejoin. To his left, the trail wound in a gentle slope through an oasis of the last trees and circled in switchbacks to the junction. The direct route, a natural rock stairway, led straight up. He paused to catch his breath and listen.

Firestone realized that he must fully consider each route before deciding. How might his choice affect his future? He had made bad choices before, decisions that led to troublesome outcomes. He scolded himself for not bringing water.

A message came to him, as if from within the Good Mountain.

Take the aggressive path up. The gentler, winding route will be easier to return upon when you are tired.

As the angle of the grade increased, his pauses between steps became longer. He felt the pounding in his heart, and a good sweat found a way through his skin. One step at a time, Firestone lifted his leg to mid-thigh height to reach a sharp rock ledge, placed the leather tread of his boot on the rock, cleared his mind, strained his thigh muscle to lift his weight, and rose like an air balloon. Confidence returned with each new height. With a step then a pause, he breathed deeply. Power filled his lungs.

Time vanished as he slowly exhaled. He gained new perspective from an expansive, yet continually changing vista. He closed one eye, then the other, and imagined that the earth revolved around him at this very spot in the universe.

Firestone thought of his grandmother. The way she snuck a swig from her small, coppered bottle of 'rheumatiz' med-cine' while quoting King James loosely with the aid of the Canadian whiskey. Like a bell on a new morning, one of her favorite Bible quotes rang through his thoughts.

Judge not and be not judged.

He chuckled at life's contradictions. His Grandmother Ada hid booze in a medicine bottle for appearance's sake. And his own, to pick and choose between dollops of religion, like greens from a salad bar, to find food that might fulfill his mind's raving hunger.

Above the tree line, around a bend, a young woman with long braided hair rested on a rock. An apparition? But she drank from a canteen, looked out at the southern panorama of rolling plains rising into the Paha Sapa, and at the same time, watched as Firestone climbed toward her. He tried to reconcile what he was seeing.

Angels, like spirits, come in many different shapes and forms.

Firestone reached a small plateau and rested on a rustic rock worn to a bench by time. Souls that had preceded him had balanced a flat stone upon a boulder wedged into the side of the mountain rock. He looked out upon the country in each of the four cardinal directions. Where he had been hot, the cool north wind cured his discomfort.

He considered turning back when again he saw the form of the young woman, lithesome, and attractive, with braided dark hair flowing down her shoulders. She returned his gaze. The world grew small. He forgot his quest. He ignored the rest of the world. He stood like a stone statue, focused on the thoughts that the woman sent through the air.

I might have missed her if I had taken the easy path.

She edged her way down the steep trail from the summit while he waited on the plateau, the only place wide enough for two people to pass. The woman was real. Her broad, confident but crooked smile captivated Firestone.

She reached out a hand. "Sally," was all she said, and she continued on her way.

She seemed to know that in time, having felt her touch, he must follow.

Firestone regained his composure. He needed to complete his climb. He crawled over a landslide of slippery, crushed slate and imagined sliding a thousand feet into the crevice below. Higher and higher he ascended, grasping a handhold wherever he found one. Finally, he pulled his weight up and over the ultimate ledge and reached the top of the broken trail.

He leaned against the mountain slope and stared at the sky. A falcon flew from an unreachable perch above him, swooped in a large arc out over the checkered plains and circled back. He called out to the young woman several hundred yards below.

"Look!" His yell echoed through the canyon.

Through a timeless distance, Sally smiled back before bouncing away. Her face revealed that they had shared something special.

The falcon flew dangerously close, directly at Firestone, as if staring, before he swerved in the air currents.

A mountain bluebird whistled from a nearby rock, an arm's length away.

Firestone listened to the sweet melody and envisioned his earthly troubles, his guilt, his doubts, and his fears turn to particles of dust and disappear into the sky.

Words of a favorite song faded into the wind while he worked his way down the Good Mountain. He relished each step, fulfilled by a cool breeze. Having no extra cloth to leave on a tree, he stooped to the uneven path and found a sharp thin stone shaped like an arrowhead. On the uphill side of a southwestern overlook, a charred tree trunk grew out of the rock. He drove the stone into a thin crack in the grain of the dead but solid wood, leaving a sign in remembrance of his forebears. He turned and paused four times, north, south, east, and west, and asked for strength and forgiveness.

Peace filled his heart as he set off to find Sally.

Spearfish Creek

Firestone passed by the wooden, A-frame cabin on his way off the reservation, stopping briefly for a smoke, hoping to talk again with the Cheyenne caretaker and thank him. Finding no one around, he hiked the mile long path down to the highway. Firestone continued walking along the shoulder heading south and west. At the sound of an approaching truck, he turned to stick out his thumb while walking backwards. As the truck slowed and the driver motioned to the flatbed, Firestone looked back toward the reservation where the caretaker waved broadly from horseback.

He stayed with the truck thirty miles west where the driver pulled off for gas in Spearfish. "I'll be gassing up, then going on to Butte, Montana, if you want to ride along? A man could find work in the mines."

"Thanks, but I'll get off here. Got someone to find."

"You watch out for that 'someone,' young man." The driver grinned as he headed west.

Firestone walked into town, and hearing his stomach growl, found a café. From behind the counter, a waitress, an older woman with a friendly demeanor, asked, "What'll ya have?"

He looked over the chalkboard menu, "The grilled cheese sandwich and a glass of milk."

Firestone used the bathroom to wash the mountain's dust from his face and hands. As he sat back at the counter, the waitress set a plate down in front of him. He took the opportunity to ask, "Ever seen a pretty girl with a long braid and a crooked smile, goes by Sally?"

"You mean Sally Jane Cannan. She's a peach. Stays up the Canyon at her grandfather's cabin on Spearfish Creek."

SALLY JANE

Sally's mother answered the knock, took one look at the handsome but ragged young man, and opened the door, "I've heard about you. Call me Caroline. I'll see if Sally's available."

"Thank you, Missus Cannan."

Firestone could hardly believe his good fortune. Sally greeted him with a long hug as if they had known each other their whole lives. He set his gear down and she grabbed him by the hand, pulling him back out the door.

"Let's walk. Mother, we'll be back for supper."

"Careful, young lady," Caroline called out as hand in hand, the couple bounded down the hill toward Spearfish Creek.

Firestone could not take his eyes from the long braid that hung nearly to Sally's plump bottom. Her hair must have taken years to grow. They found a seat in a secluded glen where the grasses grew sparse with the coming autumn. Sally's green eyes glistened as wispy clouds gave way to the sun. They relaxed watching the clear creek water roil and rush between boulders. Her touch electrified his emotions. Firestone embraced Sally and she did not resist as they kissed for the first time.

"Where's your father?" Firestone asked, hoping for the kind of answer he received.

"He's a Navy man, a rough and tumbled sailor. We don't see him much, but he sends his pay once a month. We have a small, two-bedroom bungalow near the ocean outside San Diego. Mother and I will be going back soon for the winter."

"What about the cabin here?"

"I could live here forever, but Mother keeps returning to the coast, waiting for my father to settle down. My grandfather built the cabin and put money in trust to keep the place up."

For the next week, they hiked and fished and grilled their catch. Caroline made Firestone a bed on a squeaky couch on the screened sleeping porch and watched over the door to the house in her own light sleep.

The coming cold of October marked the time for Caroline and Sally to return home to San Diego. Caroline rolled her eyes at the young lover's plans and scoffed when Firestone promised to come west for Christmas.

Firestone caught a train back east to Chicago, and then bummed his way to Michigan and his grandfather's farm. Corn dried in the fields as the days grew shorter. Firestone worked the combine and tractor by day, and in the dark, watched the Northern Lights flicker, his dream-self surrounded by Sally's tumbling braids.

Edge of the World

After Thanksgiving, with the harvest in and a few dollars in his pocket, Firestone set out to California. He boarded a bus in Port Huron, Michigan, bound for St. Louis. After a cramped and bumpy fourteen-hour trip, he slept on a wooden bench while waiting for the eight o'clock transfer, the Route 66 Special to Los Angeles.

Firestone's rampant anticipation grew with the colorful solitude of the New Mexico desert. Such beauty; had Sally seen this? He wanted to show her everything, to travel and see the wonders of the west.

As the dawning sun lit the western horizon, Firestone noticed highway signs indicating the turn-off to the Grand Canyon. Though anxious to reach California, he walked forward through the rolling bus, and asked the bus driver, "Sir, could a guy get off here and get back on tomorrow's bus?"

The driver eased to a stop at the intersection and handed Firestone a transfer ticket, "Be here the same time. The bus runs every other day."

Firestone grabbed his possibles from the overhead rack, thanked the driver, and set out for the eighteen-mile hike north to see the Grand Canyon for the first time.

The long approach from the south gives away no clues. Pine forests line the road, and the relatively flat terrain seems to go on for miles. Firestone wondered at his decision to detour, but once he made up his mind, he always pushed ahead regardless of the consequences. His legs grew weary from the long hike.

As the short daylight of early December began to wane, the trees thinned before giving away to rocky desert. The sky opened and he quickened his pace onward to what appeared to be the edge of the world.

He came upon the rim in the forty-five degree light approaching sunset and beheld a miracle.

There are places in this world where a great spirit has touched the earth. Listen quietly, and God will speak to you.

The emptiness of the air above the Canyon caused a sense of vertigo. He wondered at the sensation of flying before backing away quickly. The river that had cut the Canyon over eons flowed far below like a ruby necklace. He lingered near the edge until dark before finding a spot several yards away from the rim to make camp. He lit a fire for warmth against the clear December evening. He savored the last half of a ham and cheese sandwich saved from the last rest stop. Using his pack for a pillow, he laid back and stared at the stars of the winter sky.

"Are you trying to start a forest fire?"

Firestone shook himself awake at the intrusion to a pleasant dream. He looked up to see a Forest Service Ranger staring back at him.

"Up and at em', let's get this campsite cleaned up. I have an appointment in Kingman I need to get to, and I don't want the park burning while I'm gone."

Firestone introduced himself and quickly began to remove the traces of the fire. "I didn't know I couldn't make a fire. I just wanted to see the Canyon. I've got to get back to the highway to catch the bus."

"I'll do you one better. The bus stops in Kingman, I'll drop you there."

At the café near the bus stop in Kingman, Arizona, Firestone splurged on Huevo Rancheros. He had never had eggs like that before. The yolk ran through a warm tortilla and covered the beans and onions and bright red peppers like gravy. The ranger had driven through the night on the seventh, and on this morning, December the eighth, nineteen-hundred and forty-one, his breakfast was cut short by the voice of President Roosevelt speaking over the radio.

Firestone received his calling to serve his country in a diner in a dusty town in Arizona. The word *infamy* rattled in his head.

EBB TIDE

The bus ride across the Mohave Desert gave Firestone time to think. Staring out the window, he wondered at a lonely Joshua tree growing from arid, rocky ground. Grandmother Ada's bible lessons came to mind, "And the walls came tumbling down." He closed his eyes to catch some rest.

Firestone awoke to the brightest sun he had ever seen reflecting a myriad of sparkles over the Pacific Ocean. He had discovered another edge of the world.

At the Los Angeles station, he bought a ticket to San Diego on a bus leaving at midnight. He wandered the streets near the station to mark time, but soon found himself uncomfortable in a foreign environment after dark. The sky held no stars, and the concrete pavement hurt his feet. He debarked in San Diego and collapsed on a bench at the bus station to wait for the dawn.

Firestone opened his eyes to a poster on the wall. An old grey-haired man wearing a top hat adorned with stars and stripes pointed a bony finger in his direction. Just down the street, nearly a hundred men formed a line waiting their turn to see a Navy recruiter. Firestone fell in place.

Later that afternoon, he knocked on the door of a small, two-bedroom bungalow near the ocean. Sally pushed open the door, walked on the stoop, and swung her thin arms over his shoulders. They kissed as only young lovers can.

Firestone whispered in her ear, "Three days. I report for my physical in three days."

Bittersweet forays into the golden hills with views of the Pacific occupied their time. Sally packed aged cheese and a stick of Genoa salami. Firestone found a dry red wine at a roadside shop. On a blanket in a secluded eucalyptus grove they lounged and picnicked. In a lasting embrace after lovemaking, they avoided talk of an uncertain future. Firestone dreaded what he knew would come, but kept his fear hidden. He left on the fourth morning, with a long kiss to remember her lips, and as he pulled away from the grasp of her hands, Firestone asked Sally to wait.

Beyond here there be dragons.

Hidden Scars

Firestone never completely forgave the Japanese for bombing Pearl Harbor. He knew that harboring hate killed the bearer, yet he could not reason himself into trust. The gruesome death of young boys imprisoned in the holds of ships gave him recurring dreams of drowning.

Sand worked into every crevice of his body. Saltwater penetrated his boots, and he felt a pinch in the muscles of his right shoulder from the weight of his pack. The surreal whirr of bullets contradicted a seagull with spindly legs that hopped inch by inch toward a crab carcass.

I think, therefore, I am.

Firestone never considered giving up, not after Sicily, well especially not after Sicily, where the homemade wine flowed like blood when the Allied troops marched into Parma. Lying in the sand, working his way to the safety of dune grass, he thought of Sally, of getting home, and growing grapevines in the fruit country of Northern Michigan. Sally would paint all day long, with smart and gentle dogs at her feet. His yellow lab would stay close, lay in the shade while he tended the garden, walk with him through hay fields, and put up a ruffed grouse or cock pheasant in the fall. And horses, they would keep horses, and together admire the animals' muscular beauty running and kicking and rolling in the spirit of life.

A haunting whistle whizzed too close. A thud. He grabbed a young Marine by the collar and dragged him to shelter beneath the beach head. He placed his palm on the wound, not fatal, not if he could control the bleeding. The hot sun enlightened peach fuzz on the boy's face. His moves must be surgical and timely. Once he released pressure, he had only moments to pull off his canvas pack, unzip the correct pocket, open a bandage, and reapply pressure. A cadence,

Keep your eye on the target. Stay alive.

War embodied no reason. War made no sense, except perhaps to cull the population.

Firestone had resisted the dehumanization of Navy boot camp.

He knew the cause was just, but his right to be an individual was also justified. His Company Commander at Petaluma saw the brightness in Firestone's eyes. He knew the lad was smart, too smart, he thought too much, and his test scores.

"Damn, the boy is a natural leader; could be an officer, might order me around one day."

But after graduating boot camp, Firestone put in the paperwork for Corps School. He wanted a non-combatant red cross on his ID card.

After Sicily, his Marine unit had received orders to the Pacific theatre, where the Americans slogged through the surf, landing upon island after island. Where, as soon as a stronghold was gained and a field hospital established, his unit moved on to the next beach. Firestone did not mind moving on. He would rather patch a wound in the field than saw off an arm or leg under some tent.

His Marine unit had established another nameless beachhead. He lay still on a cot with a burning sensation in his back. The surgeon made his rounds of the tent.

"Well Firestone, you've done it this time. You have a tiny fragment of shrapnel embedded in the muscle. Too close to your spine to operate here."

"Well Doc, what are my options?"

"Chances are that your body will mend around the metal. Hate to you lose you in the field, but your war is over. You're on the next transport home."

When the Navy troop ship hit heavy weather in the North Pacific, Firestone strained his legs against the bulkhead to keep from rolling off the bunk. In a fitful attempt at sleep, he dreamed of a piece of land in the northern hill country of Michigan.

In a full sun on a cool March afternoon, he pruned grapevines with a yellow dog watching at his side. Sally waved from the porch, calling him in for a warm tuna casserole.

He awoke to a buzz running through the ship. Over the 1-MC the Captain announced, "The Japanese have surrendered."

Firestone prayed for President Truman. *Such a monumental burden to bear.*

These new catastrophic bombs brought the world to her knees. Firestone knew something had gone inherently wrong with mankind. But he also knew that a million American lives would be saved.

Keep your eye on the target, to get home.

California Coast

A harbor tug nestled the troop carrier into the pier at the Treasure Island Naval Base. The Golden Gate was the prettiest sight he had seen since Sally's tearful face on the stoop the day he left for the war. Four years, and now the Navy planned to muster out his unit. All the letters, late back and forth, all the delayed dreams, the time had come to resume his life.

Years of worry and stress disappeared when Firestone stepped off the blue Navy bus at the Embarcadero. Some unseen force untied his straitjacket. His gait grew lively. He took in a deep breath of foggy sea air that tasted of freedom.

Sally had spent most of the war in Spearfish Canyon, safe from the paranoid threats of invasion on the west coast. She remained at the cabin in the Hills, not yet knowing that Firestone had returned. Pocketbooks opened with the Allied victory, and her watercolors of the Black Hills had begun to sell. Her mother, Caroline, passed on in 1943, but her grandfather had left enough in a trust to pay the bills and keep the cabin going. She also received a small stipend from the Navy. Her father had been killed in the sea battle at Midway.

Firestone returned from war with a vengeance for life. He shot a letter off to South Dakota telling Sally he would send for her as soon as he was settled. He wanted to be able to take care of her properly. But behind the words she would find a hidden plea, *Please come quickly*.

Determined to make a mark, he enrolled at California Polytech, a few hundred miles down the coast from San Francisco. He had saved all his pay from the Navy and found a small room in a boardinghouse several blocks from the ocean. He lived frugally. After years of shoulder-to-shoulder company, Firestone relished being alone but kept his ears tuned for a friendly knock on his door. He advanced quickly through the undergraduate mathematics curriculum by dedicating his existence to study.

Sally received Firestone's letter nearly two months after his discharge. Frustrated, and without a telephone, she understood the meaning behind the words and began packing away her paintings to protect them until she could return. She folded a few sets of clothes into a leather satchel and headed for Rapid City and the train. At the station, she mailed a postcard with a photograph of Mount Rushmore: *I'm on my way.*

After a particularly grueling week of tests, Firestone walked the four blocks to the ocean. He took off his shoes and felt the sand between his toes. A cold rush of tide turned him away from the Pacific. He looked up toward the highway and recognized an unmistakable profile, the one he had left so long ago. Sally set her bag on the sand and watched him walk, nearly stumbling in his haste toward her.

Had the war changed the young man she hardly knew?

Firestone splurged on a hotel room. They swam in a pool for the first time. Hand in hand, the couple walked paths along the cliffs that bordered Morro Bay and watched the ocean surf crash on the rocky shores below while sipping on a California Pinot Noir. And later, in a lolling, loving caress, time had not passed at all.

When Firestone left the hotel for his Monday morning classes, Sally purposefully walked the streets and found a nice upper flat with an ocean view.

We must have a proper kitchen and a large front picture window for my easel.

While Firestone studied, Sally took her watercolors to the seashore. Passing tourists readily bought her light and airy landscapes. By days end, she had returned to the flat to greet Firestone at the door, where the pleasant wafts of home cooking soothed the stress from his senses.

Graduation

With all their possessions in the back seat of a 1938 Chevrolet, the couple headed back east along Route 66. Sally and Firestone stopped the first night at an old brick hotel in downtown Kingman, Arizona. In the morning, Firestone took Sally to the café where his life had drastically changed in December 1941. He yearned for another taste of huevos rancheros. He smiled as Sally covered her tortilla with the hottest of sauces. Firestone preferred mild, fresh tomatoes.

The waitress happily directed the young couple toward the courthouse in the dusty town. She followed along to serve as witness while the Justice of the Peace read Firestone and Sally their wedding vows. She signed the certificate, *Stella*, like the nametag on her white cotton uniform.

Sally had never seen the Grand Canyon, and true to his intentions, Firestone wanted to show her the splendor of the west before returning to Michigan. Both were anxious to drive east but spent a pleasant afternoon picnicking on the edge of the world. They drove on through one night and another, arriving at the Cabin on Spearfish Creek before dark on the third day, in time to walk down to the creek and catch a brown trout to grill for supper.

Sally crated up the paintings that might sell back east, while Firestone drove into Lead to see an old friend about buying a single axle trailer to tow behind the Chevy. He planned to trade the whole outfit for a new Ford pick-up truck back home in Michigan, where men knew their cars.

A Changing Landscape

Firestone had readily accepted an offer from the agricultural college in East Lansing, Michigan, to complete a graduate degree while being paid to teach undergraduate students. He looked forward to getting back to the forests and streams where he felt so comfortable. A two-hour ride east from the school and he could begin working on a house on a twenty-acre plot overlooking the Black River, the plot handed down to him by his Grandpa Arnold.

War scars a man's perception of the world.

In his absence, his grandfather had passed on, and his uncle had grown too old for the daily rigors of farming. His father, John Milton, and his Uncle Doug had begun to split off two-and-a-half acre plots from the family farm in St. Clair County. The post-war economy boomed in Detroit, known as *The Motor City*, and many young, motivated executives strove to join a new, landed gentry class. Cookie-cutter, brick mansions stole the landscape from endless, orderly rows of corn.

In the time before factory farms, Ike's agrarian-favoring government began the Land Bank Program. America's Midwest produced too many grain crops, too much corn, and too many sugar beets. The exchanges became flooded with overages, and the price farmers received dropped steadily. Forward-looking farmers began to understand the benefit of rotating crops, perhaps saving some rich, black soil for coming generations. Firestone saw the value in such thinking, but both his ailing father and aging uncle could make more money by doing nothing. In short, the government paid landowners not to farm.

The passing of time alters a man's future.

The influx of people and the tendril-like expansion of the Detroit suburbs toward farm country made Firestone feel claustrophobic. He wanted to raise his family in the country, with country values, close to nature. Something nagged at his subconscious but rose to the surface one morning at his uncle's breakfast table. Firestone realized that he didn't like the taste of the water that came from the family farm well.

On an early December trip to the highland country of northwest Michigan, Sally and Firestone found their perfect place. Eons of wind blowing sand sixty miles across Lake Michigan formed sand dunes for several leagues inland from the freshwater sea. Over time, birch, white pine, and popple forests developed along protected ridges. Streams cut paths and carried nutrients that helped to develop rich topsoil over the sand bases that provided good drainage. Lake Michigan warmed in the summer months and held the heat in the air well into September, allowing for a longer growing season. Cherry trees, both sweet and tart, and many varieties of apple trees flourished in this environment. And later, grape vineyards shared the slopes with other fruits.

A friend had suggested a section of land that bordered other large family farm parcels. Forest ridges and streams separated ownership and provided the privacy that Firestone relished. They walked the ridges and fields in a floating December snow and knew without speaking, *this is where we will raise a family.*

Firestone received a modest start from the sale of his twenty acres in St. Clair County. He invested the profit and all his savings in this section of land in Northern Michigan up near the resort town of Petoskey.

Sally and Firestone lived for the weekends and the long summer break from academia. They traveled north at every opportunity. At first, Firestone mowed out a small rectangle from hay grass. They set up an army surplus tent and camped, moving the campsite a hundred feet this way then fifty feet another before deciding where to place their house.

Firestone often walked the woods down to the trout creek, where he sat and pondered the joy of nature. Sometimes Sally came along, or other times when Firestone worked the land, she walked alone. Sally often felt a presence nearby and occasionally thought she saw an old man walking through the orchard in the distance beyond the stream. A red-winged blackbird might shriek, or a doe might start and bound away. And when she looked again beyond the stream, the figure disappeared.

"I thought I saw an old kindly man walking in the orchard today."

"How could that be?" Firestone replied.

Firestone completed his Master of Science Degree in Finance in 1948, and they moved Up North permanently, away from the hustle and stress of the city. Together they built a cabin in a clearing in a hay field, near a trout stream in the highlands of northern Michigan.

Up North

Sally's watercolors took on the new panorama of northern Michigan: the sandy dunes and blue lakes, the deep snow of winter, the first gentle green buds of spring. Firestone planted grapevines and tilled a large vegetable garden. When the afternoons warmed, he walked through the woods down to the creek and cast to a hungry brook trout for supper.

Business boomed throughout the country and land was inexpensive. Industrialists who had profited from the war bought up the pristine waterfront and built Victorian cottages to spend a few weeks each summer away from the city heat. The air around Petoskey was said to have healing properties.

One mid-June day, he and Sally packed a lunch, loaded the canoe into the white Ford pickup truck and set out to spend the day floating down the Jordan River. She was an able paddler and at times even took the rear seat so Firestone could fish from the bow. They tied the stern of the canoe off near the Webster Landing and drifted on a manila line with the ease of a wood duck paddling beneath the surface. Firestone cast to a deep hole in the bend while Sally sketched with a pencil on the pad she always kept nearby.

Until Sally heard a rustle in the grass on shore, they did not know they were being watched.

A booming voice called out, followed by the splash of waders tromping into the river. "Hello, there," can you show me how you catch those trout? Happy to pay you."

Naturally, the noisy fuss ruined the hole. "Well, I could have," Firestone replied dryly.

The intruder, a Mr. George Blackwood from Memphis, Tennessee, stood in the river nonplussed, dressed in the latest garb from a fancy shop in Chicago. His driver looked on from shore while polishing a shiny, black Lincoln Continental.

Blackwood was insistent, not used to being disappointed. Firestone stepped out of the canoe in water to his knees and pulled Sally to shore.

"Well, the first thing you need to learn, trout do not respond to noise."

They rested together on shore while the pool settled. Blackwood offered them a smoke from a silver case. Sally declined and walked further up the bank with her sketch pad. After a couple cigarettes each and the trading of necessary facts, Firestone suggested that Blackwood observe. He waded skillfully back into the stream holding his bamboo rod in his right hand. He pinched an Adams fly tight to the rod. He stood still, careful to avoid casting a shadow over the hole. After a minute or two, he took one false cast, and on the second, laid his fly just upstream of the deep run. The fly floated down into a riffle. He raised his wrist as a fish gobbled the fly.

Firestone returned the trout to the river and walked back to where Blackwood watched from shore.

Blackwood had not built a fortune by being stupid. Dumbfounded by the natural ease of this young man, he took a deep breath and walked into the river. He repeated everything he had seen in the same order. Except that his back cast slapped the water, and on his forward motion, the line tumbled over his shoulders and the hook caught on his fancy vest.

Sally's sketch caught the garbled line midair. Blackwood laughed at her caricature and waded back to try again.

"Slow down, now, relax," Firestone suggested.

On the third cast, a trout hit the fly.

They made a deal while smoking on the riverbank. "I have a proposition. Maxwell can give Sally a ride home and meet us at the launch near town. I'll float down with you, and you can teach me how to fish.

He handed Firestone a hundred-dollar bill. "Still backed by the gold in Fort Knox."

Maxwell met them at the takeout just south of the town of East Jordan. He helped Firestone pull the canoe from the river and tie it down on the roof on the Lincoln. Blackwood carried a full creel, including a trifecta, a twenty-inch Brown trout, a twelve-inch Rainbow, and the rare prize, a fourteen-inch Brook trout.

On the float down the river, Blackwood had offered Firestone a job. "Take care of my summer place for me. Hire out whomever you need for cleaning, maintenance, whatever. I'll pay you well. And my wife's family has a place down in the Georgia barrier islands. We need a good man there, too."

Back at the cabin, Sally pan-fried the day's catch and insisted that Maxwell join Firestone and Mr. Blackwood at the picnic table. Blackwood raised his eyes but quickly realized he was no match for Sally Thompson.

"Y'all will love the barrier islands."

Chapter Four:
Hurricane Harriet
1962-1964

SALTWATER

A black hole, he pondered in a way beyond his twelve years. Samuel heard a famous singer describe the loss of her father as entering a black hole. He understood her meaning but carried on with his life, putting such emotions aside.

No use worrying about something that cannot be changed.

Yet, in a clinical manner, he thought about his mother often. He snuck a look at pictures in a leather album that Firestone kept hidden in a drawer. She had been pretty, almost fragile. He wondered how a socially awkward man like his dad had wooed and won her. Samuel's sensitivity had certainly come from his mother. Firestone must have changed after Sally died, when he became both father and mother.

A man must adapt to the curves that life tosses his way.

Samuel learned early of the healing properties of ocean water. He noticed how cuts and scrapes from his land adventures disappeared when he rubbed sand from beneath shallow ripples on the wounds. His hair, already blond, bleached out in the sun, and his skin turned brown. He walked the beaches for hours and lost track of time while kicking up the surf. He became a strong swimmer on his own, swimming not being one of Firestone's strengths, nor a skill that he taught his son.

And his father worried, and warned, "Watch for the tidal currents, especially at the ebb tide, son; strong currents can carry a man all the way to Scotland."

But Samuel struck out on his own at every chance he could get. He ventured further each time and discovered the limits of the island. And once the sea border became too confining, he taught himself to sail.

The sloop had not moved from the boathouse for many years. His father had taken the wooden craft in on a business trade from a shady New York banker who housed his mistress over on Amelia Island. Firestone set up the purchase of a small marina on the southwest end of St. Simons for the banker and handled the paperwork for the lady friend who acted as titular head of the corporation. She hardly ever took time away from sunbathing to visit the marina. In addition to the title to the sloop, Firestone received an envelope each month with twelve crisp one-hundred-dollar bills inside.

Samuel watched from shore while sailboats with full crews skipped between barrier islands, seemingly without effort, like white-winged birds. He watched as most motored into the marina with sails down, and the fancy owners hopped off gracefully while the crews cleaned up. He watched intently when more skillful captains entered port under sail using all the forces of nature, including the wind and current, with an innate understanding of the dynamics being placed upon the vessel to bring the boat alongside the pier. He hungered for that knowledge. He yearned to fly upon the water.

He read, and studied, and watched, and one day, without asking, he rigged the mainsail ready to haul, pushed the sloop down the boathouse tracks, and held tight to a bow line as the sleek wooden craft floated free in brackish water.

On a sunny, early September day, he hopped aboard the sloop. Fortunately for the inexperienced boy, the ebb approached slack water, and a light breeze blew in from the southeast. He pushed the bow off a wooden piling, began to gather in the sheet, and watched proudly as the main sail rose. He held the sheet in his left hand. Without a conscious effort, his right hand searched for the tiller. A gust filled the white canvas. As if being carried by a ghost, the sloop reached a balance on a starboard tack, and a burgeoning sailor guided his craft seaward through the channel.

Courier

As he struggled into adolescence, Samuel spent more and more time on the water. Whenever able, whenever Papa Firestone didn't have an errand for him to run, he would push off the bow and let the breeze take control. The moment of leaving the dock never lost allure as another adventure awaited.

Samuel's legs learned the buoyancy of the sea. He moved with athletic certainty from dock to boat, from port to starboard tack beneath the boom, and from the tiller to the bow to free a caught-up line. His arms and legs and face tanned, and his blond hair bleached white, forming a contrast with his white canvas shorts and faded blue-jean shirt.

Commercial fishermen who made a living out of the marina met his eyes and waved as he passed their shrimp pots. No wealthy, vacationing swell, the boy could handle his rig. He had the makings of a sailor.

Back at the shrimper's co-op, Old Marge ran the show. Widowed by a shrimp boat captain who had been lost with his boat during a hurricane, she made a living by buying and selling the daily catch, twenty-count to the pound. Marge was as grizzled as wave-worn, barnacled pilings. Her hair grew wild in an unnamed color, like the sea grass that hung and flowed just below the flood tide and dried and stunk in the ebb. But her smile was genuine, and when she greeted Samuel in a gravelly voice, he knew he had found a soul he could trust.

"Been watchin' you sail that wooden rig young man; seem to know what you're doing."

Samuel had stopped for a pound of fresh shrimp. He planned to surprise Papa with pink shrimp in bay seasoning. He'd make up a cocktail sauce out of bar-be-que, Worcestershire, and fresh horseradish. *What's-dis-here sauce*, Papa called it.

"I could use a boatman like you," Old Marge offered, "to run supplies to the fleet. Pay ya out of the catch, and all the shrimp you can eat."

So it was that Samuel, before his fourteenth birthday, began running his sailboat up and down the coast, from the Savannah River and Tybee Island, all the way south to the St. Johns River, where the massive shadows of aircraft carriers tied up at Mayport dominated the horizon. He particularly liked the protected waters around Cumberland Island, where dolphins quietly accompanied his wake. He felt safe in their presence and learned early that these muscled mammals portended good fortune.

Meeting

Strands of her long, golden auburn and black hair broke through the translucent surface. Beads of salt water rolled down her temples. She ran both hands through her hair while suspended, her tanned body seemingly buoyant from the waist. Plump breasts stood taut and angled slightly outward toward her arms.

He had sailed *Wanderer* over to see the ponies, to watch from the sea, to feel their curiosity as they whinnied, stomped, and shook their manes. The ponies looked seaward as if remembering the ship that brought them to this island home. Somewhere deep in their shared memories the ponies had run free over harder ground, over vast plains that extended the limit of the known world. Samuel often sailed to this deserted stretch of beach and thought of it as his own. But now he felt like an intruder.

Angelique stood confidently in the waist-deep surf, opened her emerald green eyes, and smiled at the boy in the sailboat. She placed her hands on her bare hips as if daring the boy to look away.

Samuel fumbled with the anchor line, but unable to avert his gaze, dropped the manila braid back into the water. He stood mesmerized. He wanted to jump in.

Angelique laughed and dove. Samuel watched her underwater shape grow closer. Like the dolphins he knew and called by name, this creature blew to the surface, rising as if propelled, and rested her folded arms on the side of the sloop. Her breasts were hidden by the sweep of the hull.

"I've been watching you," she said, "me and the ponies. They like your spirit."

Storm Warnings

As muggy summer eased into the gentle breezes of early fall on the barrier islands, Samuel replayed his visit to the Cumberland Sound over and over in his head. He had not told anyone about his encounter with a bronze, mermaid-like creature. In the deep recesses of balmy summer nights, where alone with his books, he finally turned off the reading lamp that hung on the headboard, he knew where the darkness would lead. And for a time, the memory would recede and hide in that place below the surface, where feelings are stored like cans of soup in a pantry.

Old Marge had kept him busy with work, and Samuel had stashed away his earnings. His dad had been away most of the summer, fixing up the cabin in Northern Michigan. Firestone had asked Samuel to go with him, but the young teen had an independent streak. Samuel, driven to work, wanted to earn his own way. Firestone had not hesitated to leave the boy alone on the island. A certain trust had developed between them. Samuel could take care of himself.

Mostly, Firestone had wanted company up in Michigan on the hot nights in late June when he would sneak away to the Pigeon River to fly fish for the big browns that came out when the hexagenia fly hatched. Firestone still fished alone at night. The Pigeon ran deep, and dark in spots where a slip might fill a man's waders. But that was the challenge, the reason to visit places where he knew no one else would bother him.

Mortality, Firestone mused, to be reminded of one's mortality, to reconnect with the innate urge to fight for life.

And he wanted Samuel to reconnect with the joy of fishing small, out of the way streams for brook trout. But Samuel had not gone fishing often, with his courier business growing strong. The boy had learned to sail the sloop on his own, so much better than his father. Firestone had given the boat to Samuel, whose first act had been to name the wooden sloop. The hand-painted gold leaf script stood out in three dimensions, and spelled, *Wanderer*.

And what a sailor Samuel had become. Whenever Firestone stopped by *The Catch*, the local watering hole, the shrimpers nuzzled up to the bar and popped for Firestone's Cuba Libre so he might listen to their tales. One evening, the Bos'n from the Coast Guard Station had regaled the bar patrons with young Samuel's exploits, "Well damn," he exclaimed, "that kid can moor that sloop without an engine better than my able seamen can handle a powered forty-four-footer!"

Despite his wishes to take Samuel north, Firestone betrayed no apparent fear at leaving the boy alone. But, of course, he was the boy's father, his lone parent, and constant worry always accompanied pride.

Samuel tossed the last mooring line to Big Mic on the *Betsy M*, pushed the bow out into the wind, hauled in the main sheet, and caught a breeze. His buddy Mickey waved, and Samuel, with both hands occupied, nodded back. He and Mickey shared a bond, both had lost their mothers young.

Big Mic, Mickey's dad, bought the new shrimp boat with the life insurance from the car accident, and felt a duty to name the boat in Betsy's memory. He had been drunk, on a bender after a week at sea. The bartender had called Betsy to fetch Big Mic, but he had insisted on driving. A wrong turn onto the St. Simon's Island Bridge, then another wrong turn of the wheel, and the truck hit a concrete post. Betsy had gone through the windshield. Her body had bounced over the barrier into the dark salt water below. A week passed before a lady walking her dog had discovered the partial remains several miles away on the beach near the old fort.

In small-town style justice, the constable let Big Mic off with a ticket for driving too fast for conditions, figuring that the law cannot punish a man more than his own conscience will in the end.

Big Mic swore off the booze for a couple weeks, then took out his vengeance on Mickey, who began spending more and more time at the Thompson place. But when the new boat had been launched, Big Mic needed his son to crew.

Samuel watched the white *Betsy M* fade into a sea green mist. He felt bad for Mickey and hated to leave him alone. A September storm was boiling in the Caribbean north of the Dominican. He and Mickey had listened to the alert on the FM radio aboard the *Betsy M* after he had dropped off supplies: motor oil, lunch meat, bread, fresh milk, and three handles of Jamison.

Big Mic had been sleeping down below but ambled up the ladder to the main deck, "Damn weathermen don't know shit. Get that blow boat off my hull. Mickey, let's head her east."

Uncertainty

Firestone had been spending his days mostly on the Pigeon, fishing the dregs of the trout season. He had also hit the big beaver pond near the headwaters of the Jordan where brookies bit like flies when the warm September sun mixed with cool spring-fed water. Firestone lived for these perfect fall afternoons in Northern Michigan, to fade into his surroundings and put aside troubling memories.

Firestone hadn't followed the news nor looked at a television for several days. Across the bend of the Sturgeon River near Wolverine, he pulled into Rocky's Roadhouse for a burger. After a couple good gulps, he nursed a beer while waiting for his food. A beeping sound and a following banner on the black and white television mounted over the bar caught his attention. He had looked up at the satellite weather photograph of a monstrous low-pressure system roaring toward the northern Bahamas.

Firestone downed the rest of the pint, threw a twenty on the bar, and headed his pickup south along Interstate-75. Stopping only for gas and coffee, he drove hard through one night and well into the next trying to reach St. Simons before the storm hit.

Old Marge counted the shrimp boats tied up in the harbor. An old chalkboard hung on the wall at the Co-Op. Her daughter Emily, the school principal, had salvaged the board and a life supply of chalk when the School Trustees had finally approved a new plastic board and erasable magic markers. Marge kept a record of every commercial boat in the sound. She recorded when boats left for sea, when they returned, and the catch they unloaded. She knew their fuel status, what they owed, and what she owed them. She owed them a lot and not in cash. Actually, most of the fishermen were in hock to the Co-op. Marge's debt was the personal kind, the kind a mother might owe a son.

Marge was the lifeblood of the local seaside community. She didn't really need the chalkboard to remember. She knew everything that happened in the small town. She knew that Old Mic had sailed east into the storm, loaded with booze, and that young Mickey was on board. She knew that Samuel often sailed over to Cumberland to see that young, bronze girl, Angelique. Marge knew Marie from the old days, and she knew the trouble that could brew up among these shrimpers when they found out the boy spent his time with the help on Cumberland Island.

Marge knew Firestone had gone back up north for the trout fishing, and he had a northern way of looking at things, a different perspective. But she couldn't be bothered with trivialities right now, a hurricane was coming.

Marge and Samuel huddled in front of the television in the Co-op and watched as Harriet skirted north of the Bahama Banks before taking an unpredicted turn west-northwest. They listened as a National Weather Service prognosticator predicted the storm would make landfall somewhere around St. Augustine, but maybe as far north as the southern barrier islands of Georgia. Firestone heard the same forecast on his truck radio near the Kentucky-Tennessee line.

In the kitchen of the big house on Cumberland Island, Marie went about her morning chores unaware of the pending storm. She avoided television, and the only station she would allow on the radio played reggae music straight from Jamaica. Out the window, she watched Angelique dancing in the garden while she picked herbs for the noon meal. She worried at the wildness of the girl but became entranced watching the young woman's fluid motion.

Angelique swayed low in her light summer dress and bent in a curtsy to the sage, as if she were bowing to Queen Elizabeth herself. She ran her slender, golden fingers through the stems and gently plucked each elongated, green leaf. She lifted the shorn herb to her face and deeply breathed in the reassuring scent.

Camille's shout from the stairway shocked Marie from the window. "Marie. Call in Hector now, we have to make preparations."

Marie yelled out the kitchen door toward the shed where Hector repaired and refinished wooden furniture. He had aged inversely with Angelique's growth. His knotty hair had turned silver, and he limped on his right leg, the result of not receiving adequate medical treatment for a break many years earlier.

"A hurricane is coming. They are calling the storm Harriet. Marie, we'll need a picnic basket for two meals. Hector, get the luggage down, and pack the Town and Country wagon. We'll be going to stay with my sister in Savannah. Need to catch the ferry."

"Savannah," Marie exclaimed, "I always wanted to see Savannah."

"Oh my, Marie," Camille replied, "You won't be going. You and Hector must take care of the big house."

Marie turned and looked out the kitchen window.

Angelique was gone.

HARRIET

After securing *Wanderer* to a protected mooring at the Co-op, Samuel made his way back to the house through a freshening wind. He screwed the wooden shutters over the windows and called in Charlie, who had been hanging around the yard. He purred for Willy, a feral tomcat, who hunted mice and other pests in the shed and boathouse. Not seeing or hearing any response, Samuel figured the cat could take care of himself, and anyway, he really didn't want the cat in the house.

Samuel wondered about his father. The phones had been out for a day, and he had also lost electrical service. He knew that like Willy, Firestone would be fine, but some company sure would be nice.

He pulled out the prewar, Martin D-18 his father had promised would be his someday. Without thinking, he fingered some brooding chords. The strumming soon grew into picking, and he found himself creating the mood of the impending storm in music.

A wax candle glimmered against the room's dark walls. He was shut in, and a feeling of being trapped overcame his better senses.

What about Mickey? And the bronze girl on Cumberland Island?

Samuel found his green, slicker overalls and jacket, called in Charlie, and set out to the Co-op, at times walking backwards in a pelting, horizontal rain.

Old Marge paced the dock master's office. Her arms fluttered up and down as if she were a bird taking flight. Static rang from the battery powered ship-to-shore radio.

"Mayday," she repeated, over and over, "the *Betsy M.*"

Samuel coaxed her to calm. He filled the water kettle and lit a propane burner. In a ceramic pot, he placed two Plantation Mint teabags and found the honey.

Still Marge was unable to sit but finally opened up, "I've been monitoring channel 16. The sea is a swirling monster. The worst down near Mayport. The Coast Guard boat was called down there."

"No one to respond to Mickey, then," Samuel said, half out loud, half to himself.

When Samuel finally cleared the sea buoy, the raging Atlantic tossed the head of the Thompson run-about back and forth like a carnival ride. In his haste to depart the marina, his knots on the extra gas cans had been tied loosely, and the containers slid and banged against the wooden hull. The Chrysler engine ran strong and roared as he climbed each wave.

The last known position of the *Betsy M* was twenty-eight miles south and east, off St. Andrews Sound. In normal conditions, an hour ride would get the twenty-one-footer to the spot where he and Mickey often fished.

Samuel held onto the wheel for balance as he steered. His sea legs bent at the knees to absorb the unpredictable shocks. The wind backed to the north-northeast. The Thompson surfed with the swells, caught up to the next one, and the bow dove. The stern became airborne, and the props roared. Over and over he fought the sea from grabbing the wheel and held on as he was engulfed in green water.

He heard the extra gas cans break loose and briefly turned as the sea carried them away. He knew these waters well yet strained to see beyond the rain pelting into his eyes. Samuel knew the wind had blown his course closer toward land and away from his target.

I need to get seaward. I have to find Mickey.

Samuel turned the wheel.

Flotsam

In the aftermath of the storm, Angelique walked barefoot along the Cumberland shore. She loved the sand between her toes but carefully avoided the flotsam. Seaweed, bits of trees and branches, and links of broken anchor chain had been driven up by the tide and left to merge with sandy mud upon the ebb.

Angelique had been wandering when the storm hit, and unable to walk back to the big house, weathered the blow in the hollowed-out base of an ancient live oak in a central island meadow. Several ponies had huddled nearby in the dune seagrasses to ride out the wind. She had fallen asleep and awakened to the sound of their hooves against the sandy earth. One particular mustang stood above the slowly waking young woman, and their eyes met for a moment before the horse bounded away.

She was driven to follow the mustang's tracks to the beach, where she received a second sign as porpoise circled in a near shore tidal current. Angelique called out to them as they dove and rose and seemed to respond. But the sea mammals swam in a purposeful manner, almost urgent, and urged her up the beach, further toward the open sea.

With her best summer dress wet and torn, she thought about returning to the big house to let Marie know she was alright. But she spotted the shiny carcass of a lap strake runabout a few hundred yards further east, where the still tide met the sand. The current would turn soon and begin to flood.

She ran the last few yards in erratic strides to avoid the sharp edges of debris. A broken boat lay on one gunnel, half buried in the sand. On the far side, partially obscured by the hull, she saw a body she recognized. The boy, the sailing boy.

She rushed to him and fell to her knees while lifting his head into her lap. She brushed particles of sand away from his tender skin. Skin, cool and clammy, but alive.

Angelique dragged the boy up the sandy slope toward the tree line and away from the incoming tide. The sun rose and warmed the sand. The trees would provide shade. Beyond the tree line she heard the whinny of a mustang pony.

Pelicans floated on the sea air like a flotilla of bombers. Porpoise fished in the currents offshore.

The boy opened his eyes.

The Big House

The morning after the storm, Marie walked about the yard filled with debris and searched the horizon. Fleeting prayers came and left, floating among the hope and despair in her thoughts. She decided to wait there, somehow knowing Angelique had survived the storm. The girl would return on her own. Anyway, she couldn't leave old Hector with his leg gashed and most likely broken again, the result of a section of the roof tearing off the big house in the wind. The partial roof lay in the grass like a raft waiting to be launched. Marie wished they all could jump on that raft and float away.

Marie dressed the leg and built a rough splint from one-by-three cutoffs wrapped with tape. She gathered wood and made a fire in the cook stove that now vented directly into the sky. She put a chicken on to boil for soup; chicken soup, good for any ailment and good for the soul. All the while, her eyes scanned the island horizon for the shape of her daughter.

The rhythmic clanking of a diesel-motored boat preceded the arrival of the *Joanie D* at the wooden dock on the Intra-Coastal Waterway behind the big house. Marie watched as a young woman at the helm, dressed in tight short-shorts and a halter top, eased the shrimp boat up against broken rafters. An older man with silvery-white hair waved to Marie. He jumped gingerly on the pier, careful to avoid the sharp edges and gaps in the decking.

"Firestone Thompson, here," he called out, "looking for my boy. We lost him on the radio in the storm somewhere near here. This is my neighbor, Ellie. The *Joanie D* is her boat. How did you folks make out?"

"Banged up a bit," Marie answered, "My Angel stayed out in the storm, but she will return, maybe your son, too. I have brewed chicken soup. Come, drink a cup."

Firestone, momentarily mesmerized by Marie's coral-brown eyes, motioned to Ellie, who was tying off the boat. He walked toward the remains of the kitchen, where Hector sat propped up against the wall, spooning carrots from the soup. Firestone saw his blood-smeared pants, and the rough splint on his leg. "We need to get you to the hospital over in Brunswick."

"Don'ya worry 'bout me, find those children."

"You take Hector, the ol' goat," Marie interjected, "nothing left here."

Firestone felt an instant kinship to Marie. He couldn't help but notice her shapely form, but her feistiness and obvious motherly instincts caught his attention. "You need to come along, too."

Ellie smiled and reached under Hector's shoulders to lift him to his feet. Firestone caught the other arm, and they walked him to the dock. Once they hoisted Hector aboard and laid him on the padded seat, Ellie covered him with a blanket. Firestone turned, motioned, and called out to Marie.

"Go on, now," she yelled, "I will stay and wait for my Angelique."

Firestone knew how the woman felt. He knew deep in his soul, but he couldn't leave her here alone. He walked back down the dock and across the yard to reason with her.

"I need to find my boy, too. We'll come back as soon as we get Hector to the doctor. There's no time if we want to save his leg."

"You go, you go," she cried, hands clasped together before she turned away.

And as she turned, she and Firestone, in the same moment, let out a communal sigh of relief, as if singing the final chorus of a gospel song.

Into the far side of the yard walked two young shapely forms, arm in arm.

"Mon Dieu," Marie cried.

Chapter Five:
Winter Breezes
Autumn 1964

Easy Sailing

Angelique tossed the last mooring line to Old Marge on the dock. Marge's grizzled smile betrayed grudging approval for the way Angelique looked at Samuel, who raised the main sail and guided the sloop out St. Simon's buoyed channel. Angelique climbed to the foredeck, leaned back on her elbows, and let the sea breeze run through her long hair. As Samuel was born to the water, Angelique seemed born to the wind.

Lives of the shrimper community began a slow return to normalcy. Though neither the *Betsy M* nor their bodies had been recovered, Mickey and Big Mic had been remembered with a party no one would soon forget. Death followed those who made their lives on the sea, like a cloud that hung always present in a background never revealed through the fog.

On the porch of the St. Simon's cottage, Marie raised Hector's cast covered leg to rest on a white wicker footstool. She rocked and enjoyed her coffee with the morning stillness. Hector complained, feeling useless, and Marie shushed him, "Enjoy the rest while you can; before long, you'll be back to work."

Missus' Camille had come by the Co-op a week after the blow looking for Hector and Marie. Old Marge had called Firestone, and sensing trouble, Sheriff Callaghan, too.

"I've come for my man and my cook," Camille announced in her aloof manner to Old Marge.

Marge heard a truck door slam in the gravel parking lot and looked out to see Firestone storming toward the door, just as Sheriff Callaghan's Bronco skidded to a stop. Camille sauntered out the door to demand her possessions.

"You do not belong here lady. You should be thrown in jail for leaving Marie and Hector in peril just to protect your house. Did you even consider Angelique?"

Firestone nearly tossed the socialite off the dock before Callaghan intervened, "Y'all go-on back north to Savannah or Charleston, or wherever. Leave those folks alone. You've done enough harm."

Camille stormed off in a huff, beside herself.
Who will cook? How will I clean up the mess back at the Big House?

In mid-October, Firestone had driven back "Up North," as he called it, for the fall grouse season, and to winterize the Petoskey cabin before returning south. Marie sensed that Firestone had to get away, for his own reasons, as well as to give her and Angelique some time to settle in, to make the cottage their home.

Old Marge stopped by to check on Marie and Hector, "Lordy, Lordy. I've never seen that Firestone so mad. I believe he would have tossed that fancy woman right into the river."

Marie took one last sip of coffee and went inside to straighten up the cottage and to prepare a mid-day meal for her new, extended family.

Safe, safe for the first time in our lives.

Samuel breezed through his schoolwork without a second thought. Emily, Marge's daughter and the school Principal, knew he was bright, perhaps too bright. Samuel became bored easily. He made up excuses to leave classes early. His teachers wanted to punish him but could not, not with his test scores. Emily knew that Samuel had a yearning for the freedom of open water. She sensed that if pushed too hard, Samuel would simply up and leave, and that would be a waste of a gifted mind.

Angelique, a natural beauty, presented a different problem. Marie had enrolled her in the school, but she slept through classes or doodled on a sketch pad. Emily saw the male teachers stare, especially Joe Hardin, who was just out of grad school and taught math, a subject that Angelique had neither aptitude for nor interest in.

So when Joe kept Angelique after school for "extra work," and Emily walked in as Angelique pulled her head away from the desk and swung at the teacher, Emily knew that either Joe or Angelique had to go.

Emily understood the drives of a virile, male teacher and she understood the confused ways of a young, beautiful girl. Angelique belonged in a safer environment, perhaps the private art academy up in Savannah where an old college friend acted as headmistress.

Angelique ran from the room and straight to the docks, her heart hoping that Samuel had not yet sailed for his courier rounds.

Emily looked at Joe, whose red face hung in shame, "Looks like I came just in time to save your career."

"I didn't touch her," Joe pleaded.

"No, but you wanted to, maybe would have. Joe, take a week off. Go see that girl from Tallahassee. Get your head back on straight."

Savannah

Angelique ambled around the park on a muggy, late October afternoon and searched for an empty bench to sketch. Inspiration for her drawings normally came from somewhere inside her, and she struggled to conform to the assignment, but she hardened her determination to try.

Papa Firestone had settled her in a student's boarding house. He personally vouched for her talent with the headmistress, and the letter from Emily also helped. Angelique wanted to make things work, but she missed Marie's warm hugs, and she yearned for Samuel, the way he understood her without speaking. She needed a place to belong.

Sailing seemed so easy with Samuel. They did not have to talk. A natural comfort rode in the air between them. She read his thoughts.

Old Marge had called Firestone upon Emily's recommendation, and he had rushed to St. Simon's Island. After settling Angel in the art school, Firestone had driven back up north to finish the chores he had left undone. Marie remained strangely silent about sending her Angel off, hoping, approving, but silent. Marie wanted the move to work out, but she understood her daughter's wild ways and her need for freedom, like the wild ponies back on Cumberland Island.

Samuel was simply heartbroken. He had not stayed to say goodbye. The night before Angelique left, he skipped the farewell dinner, and with his half mutt, half lab, Charlie, sailed *Wanderer* to a deserted beach on Cumberland Island and anchored off for the night.

Miss Marianne, the headmistress of the Savannah Women's Academy of Art, lived in the main suite of the Victorian boarding house just across the park from the school. Marianne was pretty in a prim and proper sort of way. Her dark curls never swayed in the breeze. Her round, brown eyes seemed to stare through you like a welding torch cutting steel.

When Angelique returned from the park, Marianne called her into the sitting room. She spread Angelique's sketch book out on an inlaid, mahogany table.

"Why, this is not a park bench," she whispered in a wondering manner, "this is a boy in a sailboat.

Dancer

A few nights later, Angelique tiptoed down the curved, carpeted stairwell, cut across the foyer, slowly turned the deadbolt, and quietly closed the heavy front door behind her. The weather had stayed warm for November. The close humidity of her room drove her crazy. *The boy is gone*, she thought, *as a puppy-dog might see life when caged and alone. Only now, all that exists lies here, in front of me.*

She breathed deeply and walked across the park in the darkness. She gained confidence with each step. Her leather sandals tugged at her toes. Music, she heard music. The sound grew louder as she dodged traffic crossing Bay Street and entered the park above the wharf.

Two young toughs sporting leather jackets and pointed, black shoes played splits with a switch blade in the moist grass near the sidewalk. They stood and called out as she inhaled a mixture of tobacco smoke and weed and hurried by.

Near the iron stairs that led to Lower Factors Walk, she passed a bearded bum on a park bench. He raised his head from his dingy blanket and studied her. As she began to descend the steps, following the music, Angelique heard clearly through his garble, "Don't go down there."

Angelique turned to look and saw an empty bench. A feeling came over her as she hesitated near the top of the stairway, considered the warning, then descended anyway.

I need to dance.

On the river side of the brick buildings, the wharf came to life. A pair of drunk sailors stumbled arm in arm and barely noticed as she sidestepped them. Bar fronts opened to the uneven, cobblestone street, and Angelique looked in at each scene. She studied the patrons who seemed to belong, as if in a movie set. She gravitated down the wharf and followed the music.

Past the swankier restaurants, past the trinket shops, past the store with expensive blown glass ornaments, she followed the Reggae beat, around an unlit corner, through a brick tunnel, and into a side door, where a burly, bearded bouncer checked the identification of a handsome, older black man.

The gentleman with silver-tinged hair passed through easily, then turned, and breathed in a waft of the perfume of youth.

The bouncer asked Angelique for her license, "Eighteen to enter, sweetie."

The gentleman smiled, "She's with me."

He took Angelique by the arm and led her into the smoky crowd. She broke free of his grasp and ducked beneath the outstretched arm of a man holding a beer. Lithely, she made a trail toward the wooden dance floor. She tossed her sandals to the side and began to sway along with the steel drums, as if she were part of the music.

On and on she swayed to each new song, though each one sounded much like the last. With her eyes closed, she melted into the rhythm while the men drank and watched her and ignored the singer in dreadlocks.

Behind the bar, the owner saw her effect on his customers, who stared and gulped their drinks, and returned for another round. During a break, he worked his way over to the dance floor where Angelique stood waiting for the next song.

"Frank," he offered, "I own the place," and he handed her a twenty-dollar bill.

Angelique looked at the crisp bill, then down at her feet. Her toes had begun to accumulate dust from the floor. She remembered the bum's warning, but looked up anyway.

"Angel," she replied.

Island Songs

Ellie pushed open the door to the Co-op and set a six pack of light beer on the counter in front of Old Marge. Ellie drank light beer to keep her figure. She reached for the church key that hung near the register with one hand, and with two long-necks in the other, popped the tops.

She handed one to Marge, "Firestone back from the north country yet?"

Ellie had received the *Joanie D* in her divorce settlement. She knew very little about shrimping, so she leased the boat out for a steady income. She stopped by the Co-op from time to time to check on her investment.

Marge walked around the counter, sat down in one of the two chairs by the dock window, raised her tired feet onto a small table, and took a long pull on her beer, "What y'all want with that poor man? He's nearly twice your age."

"Not twice, Marge. Not nearly twice. And he's young at heart."

Hector quickly tired of sitting around, and against Marie's better advice, set about chipping and painting the cottage. He needed a cane while walking on the ground but climbed the extension ladder like an acrobat. He kept up a regular conversation with Charlie, while the lab kept one eye on the old man, and the other watching for Samuel. Hector worked slow and steady, and always took a lunch break to enjoy whatever delight Marie had prepared. After lunch, he rested on the porch, often falling asleep, and waited for Samuel to get home from school. Together, they raked up the day's chips from the bushes surrounding the cottage. Hector had a way of beginning a conversation, then easing back on his rake and listening. The boy filled the air with questions.

Samuel bored easily with his schoolwork, and with the afternoon bell, hurried home, eager to see Charlie and listen to Hector's few, well-chosen words. When Hector did utter a line of wisdom, Samuel knew enough to listen.

"One hand for the boat, one hand for me," Hector said and smiled down each time he took a step on the ladder. Samuel pictured the ladder as a sailing ship. Hector climbed the rigging to the crow's nest.

Marie called out the kitchen window, "Careful, you old goat."

And just the sound of her caring voice took Samuel's thoughts away from chores, and into a daydream, a swoon, where Angelique leaned back against the hull of his sailboat, closed her eyes, and let the wind run through her hair.

With the advent of the Christmas holidays, the ocean had taken a turn toward cold. Activity in the shrimp fleet had slowed with the weather, a fact which reduced demand for Samuel's courier service. That was all right with Samuel. He didn't like minding the main sheet in the cold, and he missed the warm weather when he could anchor over near Cumberland and swim.

At the insurance sale for Big Mic's belongings, Firestone bought a used, twenty-foot aluminum runabout to replace the Thompson destroyed in the Hurricane. He and Samuel had cleaned the boat up, replaced the seats, and set the skiff up for near shore and river fishing. As a Christmas present for Samuel, he outfitted the boat with a new, black, one-hundred horse-power Mercury outboard.

"Aye, and your worry will turn to wrinkles if you're not careful," Firestone chided Marie.

She looked up at him with trusting, brown eyes, but Firestone read concern in every move of Marie's fine features. He knew she was grateful for all he had done, for her, for Hector, and especially for Angelique. He had become their protector, their guardian.

Firestone watched the way Marie swayed, so light and graceful, to the beat of the radio while she worked. And he ached for her touch, a touch he constantly avoided.

Firestone had come to think of Angel as his own, as a daughter. And in his puritan mind, how could he become more involved with Marie? His thoughts turned to Samuel's mother, gone these many years. He still felt guilt when looking at another woman.

Marie maintained no such inhibitions, but she was always careful not to go too far. She had become attached to Firestone, just as Angelique loved the boy.

She handed Firestone his morning coffee, the first cup with a touch of cream. She poured herself a mug and gestured to the porch. As they both turned toward the wooden screen door, a shape appeared outside. Ellie, subtly dressed in a tight, flowered skirt and a top that revealed a glimpse of her small breasts, flung open the door, and walked in without a knock, "Just in time for coffee."

Marie handed Ellie her mug, "You two go on outside now, enjoy the mornin'. Out of my kitchen, I have work to do."

Ellie wrapped her free arm around Firestone and led him toward the door. As he pushed open the screen, she turned her head back toward Marie's glaring brown eyes and grinned.

Firestone had been looking forward to some time alone with Marie, to lend his ear, and together perhaps assuage their doubts about Angel. He hoped he had done right by sending her off to Savannah. The private art school could give her advantages in life. And Samuel was too young, much too young for the wild island girl.

Firestone's thoughts turned again when Ellie placed her hand on his thigh.

Winter Solstice

Miss Marianne sat at the head of the dining room table and watched while Angelique toyed with a spoon in the jam jar. The other girls had eaten early and anxiously started on their way home for Christmas. Most came from wealthy families up in Charleston or Atlanta, privileged young ladies used to catching the train and riding first class. None had Angelique's talent, but to a girl, they all considered themselves serious artists.

With Firestone tied up in business dealings over on Cape San Blas, Ellie had readily volunteered to drive to Savannah to fetch Angelique home. She was expected at the boarding house later in the morning.

Marianne had worked her way up from a poor background, her father a housepainter, and her mother a seamstress. Raised in Asheville, North Carolina, she fought her parents relentlessly on her chosen field of study. Something practical, they had stressed. The result of her decision to study art at the University in Boone meant nights as a cocktail waitress to make tuition. Men stared and often groped as she passed with a tray. Marianne thought she had left that life behind with a socially prominent position in Savannah. And here sitting before her was a young girl much like she had been.

"You need to watch out for those men," she said. "Don't trust them, believe me, I've been where you are now."

Angelique realized that her almost nightly excursions to the wharf had not been secret. "So you knew?"

"I was young once too, you know. You've been given a wonderful opportunity here. You don't need the money. Mr. Thompson will see to that."

"I love to dance, and why shouldn't I make a few bucks, if those men want to watch?"

The doorbell sounded. Both Marianne and Angelique looked up in surprise as Ellie strode through the archway in a bright, floral print dress, put her hands on her hips with an exaggerated flare, "Well young lady, are you ready for a road trip?"

Angelique had only one suitcase, a faded leather bag that Papa had given her. The bag barely fit into the tiny trunk of Ellie's two-seat Thunderbird convertible. Ellie rode with the top down year-round except, of course, in the rain. Angelique waved from the passenger bucket seat as Ellie spun out into the Savannah traffic.

Marianne stood on the porch and listened to the squeal of the tires with competing emotions. Part of her wanted to jump into the car with the girls for some unplanned, probably reckless adventure. She sighed, walked the stairs to her suite and gathered her own suitcase for the train trip home to Ashville. She hoped that Angelique would return following the holiday break.

Angelique leaned her head back on the rest. Her long sun-tinted hair flowed with the wind. She wondered at how Ellie's hair seemed to stay in place notwithstanding the breeze, so natural, yet controlled. Ellie didn't use spray. Her entire demeanor exuded confidence, a wild sort of confidence. She knew where she was headed.

Ellie turned and smiled, "Let's make a pit stop, honey. It's cocktail hour. I want to see an old friend down at Half Moon Landings. We'll take the Islands road."

Angelique hid her initial disappointment. She yearned to see Samuel. He had not written and had hidden the night before she left. But she was taken by the promise of adventure shining in this woman's eyes.

As evening approached on the shortest day of the year, Firestone sat on the porch and worried. He didn't want to alarm Samuel or Marie, but the girls were late, several hours late. He had called for Miss Marianne at the boarding house. The answering machine message droned, "Closed for break, please call back after December 28th."

Samuel waved at his father through the dusk as he and Charlie headed off for a walk on the beach. The pair romped in the pools each day once the tide receded. On this Winter Solstice, the max ebb would arrive after dark.

He loved to walk the beach under the stars, alone with his thoughts and his faithful dog. Charlie followed the young man everywhere, though at this moment, he sniffed at crabs that crawled in the clear riverine channels eroding into brown sand.

Samuel studied the surf, the almost magical way that the lead waves arrived further and further out toward the sea. He stood entranced and stared east while the last light of day disappeared. His eyes adjusted to the dark as he avoided the glare of town. Twilight passed quickly, and the constellations appeared. The seven sisters preceded Orion and the Dog star. Samuel called to Charlie, walked to the outward-most reaches of the ebb tide, and dropped to a seat in the moist muck. They would wait together through the slack water period where the earth became level and still. And when he felt the earth tilt and the tide begin to wet his feet, Samuel thought a silent prayer to the universe and began a slow and purposeful walk back to the cottage.

The Half Moon Tavern sat on wooden stilts above the salt marsh. Ellie's spike heels nearly caught in the gaps between wooden planks that served as an entrance. A blues tune echoed from a lonesome electric guitar. Once inside, Angelique's eyes took a moment to become accustomed to the murky light.

The guitar player sat in the corner on a wooden chair and nursed a beer while he played. A hard-shell case lay spread open for tips. A couple necked in another corner, and several young men at the bar had been watching them with interest, until the two ladies walked in and diverted their attention.

Ellie dropped a five spot into the guitar case, "Play something lively. I want to dance."

She nudged into a small space at the bar between two handsome young men enjoying their beers, obviously happy to be done with work for the holidays. She called to the buxom woman behind the bar, "Two shots of tequila, please, and slice the lemon fresh. This is Angel, boys. She's with me. Touch her and you'll be sorry."

Angelique's head filled with a rush like an ascending air balloon. She felt confused and warm at the same time. The guitarist kept a beat with a boot on the plank floor. The slinky strains of his homemade, glass, bottleneck slide reverberated through the room. Ellie grabbed Angel by the hand, and the ladies sashayed to the dance floor.

Morning Blues

Samuel woke to the sound of Charlie barking out in the yard. A predawn glow illuminated the far side of his bedroom wall. He tossed off the quilt and jumped to the window just in time to see Angelique swing the door closed on the T-bird. Ellie waved before she peeled out on the gravel drive headed for town.

Angelique struggled to bend down and pick up her leather satchel. He lost sight of her beneath the porch roof. He heard the squeak of the porch screen door opening and his father's boot steps on the wooden boards. His heart sank in his chest, and he lay back down and pulled his mother's quilt up over his head. He had looked forward to this moment, though he hoped it would have been last night, before the unsettling dreams, before bare feet and soiled clothes, before Firestone's harsh tone, "Bath and to bed, young lady, we'll talk later."

Unable to sleep, Samuel bided time until the house grew quiet. He snuck down the stairs into the kitchen, cut four slices from yesterday's fresh bread, slathered together two peanut butter and jam sandwiches, wrapped them in foil, grabbed an apple, and carefully placed his breakfast and lunch into his pack. He pleaded with Charlie to stop wagging his tail against the cabinets.

Marie silently watched from the stairs as Samuel and Charlie left by the back door and hurried down the lane toward the marina.

On this lazy Saturday morning, a haze hung over the mirror-still water inside the marina's break wall. Samuel was glad that Old Marge had not yet arrived. He wanted no company, no forced conversation other than Charlie, who followed faithfully, though the look in the dog's big brown eyes searched for the usual smile from his master.

The lines holding *Wanderer* alongside the dock bent in a firm, half circle from just a hint of freeze. Samuel remembered the deerskin gloves in his pack. Firestone had the gloves fitted for his son from a doe he shot two seasons earlier up in Michigan. Samuel always carried the gloves in his pack but had never used them before. He liked the way the lining slid over his hands. He stroked the suede-like brush of tanned deer hide.

Samuel straightened the four-point mooring lines with a whip of his wrist, coiled three, and tossed them into the cockpit. He called for Charlie to jump in. With the fourth line, Samuel pointed the bow toward the end of the jetty, ran along the dock pulling the boat, and jumped in at the last possible moment, barely missing Charlie's anxious, panting head. He needed the momentum of the run to clear the still water and catch the breeze that freshened and created ripples just outside the harbor entrance.

He raised the main sail to the first trim and waited while the wind flapped canvas before taking a light hold. As *Wanderer* cleared the flashing green light that marked a rock pile at the entrance, Charlie took his normal place on the bow, raised his black nose toward the sky, and sniffed salt air as if searching for a scent to guide the boat.

A bright sun on this December morning warmed Samuel's face on the port tack he had chosen. He aimed the bow toward Cumberland Island where he might find a lee anchorage, enjoy a sandwich, and perhaps read another essay from the book by Emerson that Miss Emily had given him as an early Christmas present. She had noted one called "Self Reliance," thinking the title might pique his interest, and she was right. Samuel wasn't religious in a churchy sort of way, a trait he had picked up from his father. Since Sally's death, Firestone avoided churches, yet he never spoke openly in opposition to religion. Firestone knew that Samuel understood the omnipresent spirit of an ultimate power, but neither he nor the boy could stomach being preached at.

No one really knows.

Samuel set aside his worries as he set the tiller with a line and laid his head back to feel the full glorious rays of the sun. Charlie slept comfortably forward.

After an hour or so, indeterminate, as Samuel did not care for watches, he awoke from a light nap, and switched on the battery to the ship to shore FM radio he had installed after the last storm. He heard the keying of a microphone through static on channel 16 and the urgent direction to switch and answer on Channel 21. Curious, he switched the channel to listen in on the Coast Guard.

The signal came across weakly, but he made out the sending address, the Coast Guard Group at Mayport. He couldn't make out the reply from the Coast Guard's forty-one-foot lifeboat. Again, he heard the Coast Guard, still weak, "Pilot whales, beaching themselves… south, off Ponte Vedra Beach."

Samuel had not yet begun his approach into Cumberland. He unreefed the sail, took the tiller in hand, caught a gathering north wind, and headed *Wanderer* south toward Ponte Vedra.

Beached

Samuel smelled the rot of sea flesh from a great distance before he saw two Coast Guard lifeboats ferrying between the broad ocean beach and the Coast Guard cutter anchored a mile off shore. He sailed in close to the cutter and watched as a Coastie on a smaller boat tossed a *monkey fist* attached to a line to a crewman on the fantail of the ship. Closer yet, Samuel guided his craft until he could see the dead eyes of two pilot whales on the other end of the line. A loudspeaker boomed out from the cutter, warning, "Security Zone, Keep your distance."

The two-inch line had been looped around the tails of several twenty-foot-long sea monsters to pull them off the beach and through the shallows to deeper water. Once the whales were floated, the deck crew on the larger ship gathered the beasts into a pod, and then waited for the next delivery. The crews must have been at work all through the day, as Samuel counted over forty whales floating downwind of the cutter.

He had overheard the secure conversation on the radio. Once all the whales had been gathered, the cutter planned to tow them sixty miles out to sea to the Gulf Stream currents. Hopefully there, nature might take over the process and return the flesh to the ocean depths.

Through his binoculars, Samuel watched several more deliveries. He watched as the weight of the whales sometimes parted the rope and the tails would be retied. He watched as darkness approached, and a bulldozer arrived on the shore. He watched as the lifeboat crews headed home, and the dozer buried the last few bodies deep under the white beach sand. He watched as the cutter prepared to weigh anchor, to tow a heavy, partially submerged load to a final resting place at sea.

First one shark approached, then another. Soon four or five dorsal fins swayed between the bodies. The first shark hit a whale with brute force and ripped a piece of flesh. Samuel surveyed the acre of sea surface. He watched the swarming dance of the perfect predators. Out of the corner of his vision, far at the outward, upwind end of the tied pod, he saw a different movement. He saw a whale attempt to roll.

Samuel called the cutter on the radio, "Aye there, Coast Guard, a whale is still alive."

"Sailing vessel *Wanderer*, depart the area. You are in danger."

Without thinking, Samuel trimmed his sails and tacked toward the still living whale. He ignored the repeated warnings of the cutter. He ignored the dorsal fins growing closer and closer. He slid his boat into the gap between two whales, one dead, and one very much alive. He dropped his sail and took a Swiss Army knife from the leather case on his belt. He hung over the side of his boat and began to saw away at the two-inch hawser. The whale rolled. Samuel understood the fear and longing in her human-like eye. He noticed a dorsal fin hovering closely and worked furiously. His foot slipped on the wet deck, and he nearly toppled over the side into the ocean. He caught his breath before renewing his furious efforts to cut the whale free.

Like a torpedo, a shape barreled underneath the *Wanderer* and broke the surface within inches of Samuel's arms. The dolphin landed with a slap and nosed toward the shark's dorsal fin. Another dolphin rose in the same spot and stood half in the air, guarding any approach. The shark dove and fled just as Samuel's knife parted the line. After one last mournful look, the whale rolled free, dove, and doused Samuel with a splash of saltwater.

Samuel allowed *Wanderer* to ease away from the tow as the cutter gained movement. Once clear, he raised the main and sailed into the darkening night. A pair of dolphins danced and played in phosphorescent wake.

East Beach

Samuel cast a spotted spinner into the current that flooded into Gould's Inlet. He nearly lost his balance on the steep, sandy slope that had been gouged out by eons of tides, in and out, twice a day through time unrecorded. He looked down at his ankles sunk into the dark sand, enjoying the feeling of the earth pulling him down. He focused upon the flight of the lure and the pull of the moon.

Just past low tide, sandy islands showed across the stream, and saltwater broke white in gentle surf. He had watched the sun rise and taken a few blind casts. He had come for the fishing at low tide, at the beginning of the flood, when larger fish might become emboldened and venture inside the shallow inlet. He had also come to be alone, before the beachcombers arrived, and before the families with kids who splashed and played on the flat expanse. He had come to be alone but hoped that Angelique might follow.

Two nights earlier, after freeing the whale, he had gone to anchor off Ponte Vedra Beach. He and Charlie slept soundly through the night. He awoke in the morning to the squawk of the FM radio, startled, then annoyed that the sun filled beauty of the morning had been disturbed. Firestone had been tracking his progress and knew of the whale exploits. His father had patched through on the Coast Guard frequency, and none too subtly suggested that his son return home directly.

Fighting the wind, the sail north to St. Simons had taken the rest of the day and most of the night. Samuel had docked *Wanderer* at the Co-op sometime after three a.m. and walked the mile-long path back to the cottage, following along the shore. He had quietly entered the house and heard no stirring on the wooden plank floorboards. Firestone listened from his bed and only slept when he heard the compaction of the steel bedsprings from Samuel's room.

From her second-floor loft, Angelique stared out the window and waited for his familiar shape to appear in the dull moonlight. She studied the path, for she knew Samuel would shun the road. Her lithe frame and bare feet caused no sound.

Samuel slept all through the day and the next night, only awakening to follow the flood tide to East Beach.

Angelique cut four slices from a loaf of warm, cinnamon-raisin bread that Marie had baked fresh. She placed them on the stove-top toast tin and turned on the gas. On a separate burner, she fried two eggs in butter, turning them over just past easy. A pair of cardinals played in the live oak tree outside the kitchen window. She filled a thermos with cool, just-sweet mint tea, and headed into the growing daylight with the fried egg sandwiches in a paper sack.

A lone, dark silhouette broke the early sun's rays as she paused near the clear, creek-like bypass before plunging her feet into the ankle-deep run. The shape had not turned but knew she was there.

"Breakfast," she called while coyly striding toward Samuel with an exaggerated squeezing of sand from her toes.

Samuel glanced at Angelique, then continued to reel in a small whiting. He brought the fish to his hands, released the hook, then tossed it back into the current. The rising tide had begun to cover the bar. A pair of dolphins entered the shallow river from the sea. He laid his rod down and washed his hands in the salty water, scrubbing with grains of sand.

Angelique spread a large towel, plopped down on the covered sand, and opened her pack. Samuel wanted to resist, but when she motioned him to sit, he lost all resolve. He devoured the first yolk-soaked sandwich. Angelique tore off a small corner of the second sandwich for herself and handed the remainder to Samuel. Yellow smears ran down his chin.

He gulped the gentle, sweet tea from the thermos, wiped his mouth with the back of his wrist, and realized that two days had passed between meals. She touched his thigh. He felt his desire mount, turned to face her, and leaned in.

On the early morning beach, Angelique, barely sixteen, lifted her sun dress over her head and lay back on the soft towel. Samuel, two years and a millennium younger, stood and pulled off his tee shirt. His shorts dropped in the sand.

A dolphin rose in the river current, took a fish, and dove. A pair of blood red and white ducks flew low over the water. The beat of their wings whooshed like thunder.

"Canvasbacks," Samuel whispered into Angelique's moist ear.

The warmth overwhelmed him.

Christmas Feast

Hardwood coals glowed like jewels encapsulated in a ring of bricks. Firestone had built the roasting pit in the back of the property where he could see the cottage in one direction and the ocean in the other. He tended the fire with care. He added a stick of hickory when the last maple branch faded to ash. He found the hickory locally but had hauled the sweet maple back from Northern Michigan. Suspended from an iron tripod, a twelve-pound prime rib of beef sizzled and spattered when drips hit the coals.

Firestone sat on a log and sipped the Glenlivet from a handmade clay mug, one of two that remained from the set his wife had thrown while carrying Samuel. Most had gone the way of dust. The other unbroken mug usually sat like an ornament on a shelf in Samuel's room.

Every few minutes, he stood and turned the spit.

Charlie came trotting in from the beach and nearly toppled the spit with his tail. Firestone scolded the dog but could only smile when the lesson had no effect on the lab's good nature. Samuel, who had set out to the inlet for a fish to add to the celebration, walked to the fire holding up a two-foot red snapper, cleaned but with skin and head still on.

Firestone had the fish-shaped, cooking cage ready. Samuel filled the snapper's belly with fresh scallions and sprinkled olive oil and a squeeze of lemon over the red flesh. Firestone closed the cage.

"Nice fish, lad. Should be done at the same time as the roast. Let's celebrate!"

Firestone pulled out Samuel's mug, poured in two fingers, and handed the drink to his son. "The single malt, to Dougal Dee Thompson, your great, great-grandfather, and to you my son. Aye, and this'll cure what ails ya."

Samuel raised his mug, took a sip, and coughed. "Let it roll around your tongue a bit," his father advised.

Samuel took another sip, as father and son silently watched the coals glow against the backdrop of a gathering ocean sky.

The air was chilled on this Christmas afternoon, so the guests huddled inside by the fireplace. Marie called out the back door from time to time to check on Firestone's progress. Two pies cooled in the pie safe.

Angelique half worked at setting the oak table while entertaining the group in the living room. Old Marge had come bearing a fresh crab and shrimp salad. Her daughter Emily had a more traditional Caesar salad with homemade anchovy dressing. Ellie sprawled on the wicker couch and sipped from a green bottle of Heineken, one from the six-pack she had brought, along with her special bean dip.

Hector's leg had been acting up in the cool weather, so the women urged him to sit by the fire and relax. Relaxation being against his nature, he struggled to stand with a cane and got up to see if Marie needed help in the kitchen.

The Sheriff's 1955 International Scout crunched gravel in the driveway. Joe Callaghan stepped out as always in his khaki uniform pants and open-neck shirt. His wardrobe was limited even on social occasions. Ellie sashayed out the front swing door and handed the sheriff a beer. "Firestone is out back tending the roast."

"Aye, son, have all you like, but less'll do ya," Firestone, seated at the head of the oak table, said with a smile.

Firestone popped the cork on two bottles of his sweet, homemade Pinot blend and poured the first generously. Even the young folks, Samuel and his Angel, were allowed a holiday glass. Samuel enjoyed the way the sweet wine mixed with the beef. Angelique's eyes opened wide, and she stared innocently at Samuel across the table, while she lifted one bare foot and wiggled her toes on Samuel's thigh.

Samuel put away the rare roast beef like a ravenous wolf. Something about the browned fat mixed with pink, bloodied meat drove him wild. He looked up in time to lift his glass with the others, as Marie clinked her knife against her crystal goblet, "A toast to our family and dear friends, safe together."

"And to Papa Firestone," Angel added.

"Here, here, to my old and trusted friend," the Sheriff echoed while he drained his glass and reached for the wine bottle, only to be short stopped by Ellie.

"I am humbled by my extended family. I hope you enjoy the wine. Only a few bottles left of this special vintage. I have them tucked away in the earthen cellar outside the cabin in Michigan."

Apparent by the aimless gaze in Firestone's eyes, words had been left unsaid. The air at the table clouded over. Everyone understood that Firestone recalled brewing this vintage with Sally the last autumn, before she left this world.

"For chris-sakes," Ellie slurred, having finished several beers and half a bottle of bourbon while waiting for dinner. "Time to free your memories from the shadows."

Firestone stood and sipped the last drops from his glass. The festive mood faded into dying fireplace embers. Marie raised her eyebrows toward Ellie and rose to clear the table. Firestone felt a sensual desire for Ellie, but never revealed the secrets of his heart. Disappointed by her demeanor, he turned his head and walked to the porch.

Joe Callaghan stood and helped Ellie to her feet, "Let's get you home, young lady."

Angelique steadied Hector, who limped to the porch, then she helped her mother clear. Samuel sat still and feigned to sip his wine until his arousal diminished and he was able to stand. Angelique smirked and swept his plate.

Later, when the house darkened, Marie slipped from her bedroom and entered Firestone's master suite. She stood by the window, her silhouette emboldened by a waxing moon. Her white cotton nightgown fell to her feet. Firestone swept back the flannel covers, and Marie lay her brown body next to her patron, her benefactor, and finally, her lover.

Chapter Six:
Summers Up North
1965-1968

ROBINS AND OTHER WILD BIRDS

Patches of snow hid on the north side of wooded slopes where the sun seldom visited. Early May and Spring dawdled to show herself. Awakened by the croak of a pair of Sandhill cranes floating in the sky outside his bedroom window, Firestone had waited anxiously for Samuel's term to end, for the time when he could return to his beloved north woods.

He saw the promise of renewal wherever he looked. Wild onions sprouted bright green. Wild purple and yellow buds popped out beneath overhanging popple branches at the edge of the woods. A blue bird perched on a cedar post. Frost still lingered in the ground, and the robins, who had arrived according to a biological clock, struggled to find worms in the partially frozen muck.

Firestone worried about pruning his grapevines so late. He generally cut the leads back in March, before any early buds appeared. But with a pair of sharp pruning scissors and Samuel's help, the newer Pinot vines had been cut and tied in two days. He taught Samuel the tricks of his peaceful avocation, methods that had taken him years to discover. His artful approach combined knowledge with hope, hope that the main root would grow where he envisioned, hope that the fresh purple leads would respond to his direction.

One at a time, painstakingly, they followed a vine from the root to a natural conclusion. The three-wire trellis allowed for variations, and each plant grew differently. Some buds aimed up from a lower wire, while others pointed down from above.

Squawks of geese in migration accompanied the fresh air of spring. At least once each day, he and Samuel paused in their labor to enjoy the haunting croak of Sandhill cranes whose flight carried them to great heights in search of a safe and private field to feed. As the days warmed, the robins began to happily hop while they seized a prize meal. Charlie liked to play with the birds and dashed in their direction until they took flight. And when he walked back to the arbor and lay in the sun, the robins returned to hunt unaffected.

Given his stubborn manner, Firestone had learned the vine trade the hard way. The original arbor, planted nearly twenty years earlier, still stood near the barn and still produced local hardy varieties of catawba and concord grapes. However, he had ignored the old vines, and the root stock grew hither and yon at their own behest. Gnarled characters, with wood as thick as his wrist, the vines wound up and down and over and sideways, out of any control of man. Every year, he made sweet wine and jam and came away amazed at the resilience and bounty of nature. He was determined to train the newer Pinot vines properly. He knew they would produce better with more meticulous care.

After the new vines were pruned, Firestone set out to spend a day cutting the old arbor back. He had released Samuel to wander the woods and rediscover the spirits of the wild. He knew the boy missed Angel, who would join them for the summer once her term ended at the art school. He worried that the wild island girl might break Samuel's heart.

Bundled in Firestone's frayed woolen coat, Marie carried a glass of lightly sweetened, iced mint tea. Her southern blood had not yet warmed to spring in the north country. Cool breezes rivaled the harshest winter she had ever known. She handed Firestone the glass and retreated to the cabin where the woodstove suited her. He watched her gentle steps, even as she was bundled in one of his heavy, ill-fitting winter work coats.

Firestone laid his shears aside and followed.

THE OLD MAN

He appeared from beneath the green boughs of a hemlock tree from an obscure opening where only a deer or another small animal of the forest might emerge. The sparkle in his eyes sent out a beam of light. His smile, wrinkled from years of living in the sun, allayed any fear Samuel might have had from a chance meeting so deep in the woods. Like a large but friendly dog, almost a wolf, yet clearly meaning no harm, the old man raised an open hand before gesturing toward the empty boulder opposite the stone where Samuel rested.

A red-winged blackbird shrieked from somewhere above in the leafed ceiling.

A red squirrel chattered from a hollow beech stump.

A still-spotted, white-tail fawn stared innocently while standing just yards away in the center of the old two track trail.

Samuel had ventured out into the shadowed wood to escape the sun's heat and to take a needed break from helping his father prune vines. He sat on his favorite large boulder, one large enough to rest upon without having to bend his knees. From his perch at the side of the trail, he could overlook the ravine and see the clear creek running through a black muck swamp in the flat bottom. He could see the creek change into a stream a few hundred yards further on and run through pussy willow and reed grass. Even further, Samuel knew the creek narrowed between hard-formed banks and flowed between unkempt apple trees, the remnants of a once producing orchard.

From whence had this creature come to his father's farm, to a place where no roads led? Perhaps the old man had walked from the orchard, and the canvas knapsack strung over his shoulder carried green apples?

The old man extended his lined, tanned arm. Samuel took the grizzled hand in his own, and the touch was somehow familiar.

The ancient swooshing wings of a pileated woodpecker echoed through the woods.

A burly porcupine lounged in silence on the overhanging branch of a maple tree.

The spotted fawn watched unafraid.

Samuel passed his jug of cool well water to the old man, who drank from the spout. He wet a blue kerchief and laid the rag across the back of his neck.

A whirligig spun down from a maple, propelled like a helicopter in the freshening wind.

A monarch butterfly landed on a tall milkweed plant growing wild at the top of the trail.

The spotted fawn spooked and hopped away on awkward spindly legs.

Samuel turned. The old man was gone.

A jug of cool, well water lay balanced on a stone.

Northern Ways

Marie understood the folks down south. She knew where to go and the places to avoid. She knew the right words for the right company. Her manner was evident in the way she had spoken to Camille and other white strangers. She hid in her silence, no matter how much Firestone tried to protect her. She knew whom to trust and when to keep her thoughts to herself.

Northern ways were more subtle. Marie noticed the sideway glances Firestone never saw. Everyone in the small, northern resort town deferred to him, a well-respected man, a natural leader who knew all their secrets but kept close counsel. He walked the streets openly, proud and free, with a dark-skinned woman at his side.

Marie had a seventh sense. Back home in the barrier islands, neighbors visited her in times of trouble. A few white folks also visited, fearless ones, those not afraid to admit that something more existed out there, something not visible to the everyday eye. Firestone believed in spirits. She knew he saw things he could not explain. Marie figured that his time alone in nature had taught him to listen closely to the earth and sky, to the trees and animals of the wild. Neither organized religion nor society had brainwashed her renaissance man.

And the boy, Samuel, had been born under a sign. Life came naturally to him. Marie felt his shimmer the first time they met. He walked the world surrounded by an aura, watched over by a heavenly body, his spirit mother. Marie could only try to protect him in the waking life.

Firestone had found Marie in a time of need, and her Angelique had found Samuel on the beach. The twining of their paths had been no accident.

The previous evening, Samuel had mentioned a taste for her pork barbeque stir fry accompanied by saffron rice. With Firestone away on a trout fishing trip to his cabin on the West Branch of the Escanaba River in the Upper Peninsula, Marie ventured into town on her own for the first time.

She had the keys and some minimal instruction on the classic VW Beetle that Firestone kept under wraps in the barn. Just last Sunday, they had taken a leisurely drive on Waters Road to the spot where the headwaters of the Au Sable and Manistee Rivers emanated from the same swamp. While they walked paths beneath the giant, virgin White Pines at the state park near Hartwick, Firestone had explained the route of the Native Anishnabe, sometimes called Chippewa, who in colonial times made the "Grand Traverse" from lake Huron to Lake Michigan along these two, clear trout streams. By birch bark canoe, they paddled up the Au Sable from near present-day Oscoda, portaged the short two-mile distance to the Manistee River then rode the current downstream to the plentiful fruit bearing grounds near the shores of Lake Michigan. Marie had driven all the way home and felt confident she could make the trip to town while Samuel slept in.

The Farmer's Market spilled over from the park near the lake and created a minor traffic jam on Lake Street. Marie braked hard when a pair of ladies, dressed to the nines, stepped out in traffic to cross. She forgot to depress the clutch, causing the VW to lurch to a stall. Marie gathered her composure, restarted the engine, and circled around the block to find a spot to park. The public lot was full, and she spotted a small space in a back alley.

The selection of wares, so different from the markets in the islands, surprised Marie. Bright red apples replaced mangoes and oranges. Designer glass bottles held pure maple syrup. Steam rose from fresh oatmeal raisin cookies. Potted daisies and colorful baskets hung from the roof of the open-air sheds. She reached for a fresh loaf of cinnamon-raisin bread.

"Don't touch that," admonished a heavy-set woman behind the counter.

The fancy ladies whom she had let cross, alarmed by the outburst, looked down and frowned. An indigo bunting landed on a budding maple branch that hung above the shed. Marie stared at the clerk's reddening face and bulging eyes. She noticed the way her arms swelled where a rubber hem constricted the blood in the woman's upper arms. Without a word, Marie turned and walked in the direction of the car.

As Marie opened the unlocked door and stopped to get in, a man grabbed her arm, pulled her back, and forced her up against the slope of the hood. Before she realized what was happening, the chubby, bearded man fondled her braless chest and began to rub against her bare leg. With all her strength, Marie kneed the man in the groin. He pulled back in pain and swung at her jaw with a balled fist. Her head swung back from the jarring punch, but she gathered her wits, kicked out with her heel, and sent her attacker sprawling on the curb.

Samuel woke to a waft of wild rice boiling in chicken stock. He had slept late, having stayed up talking with Marie into the evening. Sunset came late this far north. The last glimpses of light had shown through the tall red pines whose needles grew very high on the trees, allowing him to see between the orderly trunks of the second planting. Samuel often stared into the space that dominated giant shapes of wood. His logical mind knew that air filled more space in the forest than the trees, yet he wondered why the woods appeared so dark.

"I couldn't find saffron in town," Marie greeted Samuel while stirring the pot, her head turned to hide a swollen cheek. "So I used some of your father's wild, brown rice instead of my usual Uncle Ben's. Hope you like it."

On the River

Firestone awoke confused. Too many people, too many places, and too many memories swirled around in his head. Only deep breathing made the merry-go-round slow down.

He walked to the cabin's porch, lit a smoke, and stared out over the West Branch of the Escanaba River. The winding, rust colored stream flowed twelve miles, turned east, then south, and sometimes north, but generally east again before merging with the wide main branch near the Arnold Corners. He needed this time alone to gather his wits. To others, Firestone was always in control and knew the answers to tough questions. Like a rock, he appeared firm and steady, yet he understood how flowing water sanded boulders smooth, wore them down, and softened sharp edges. As he grew older, he seemed to understand less and wonder more.

Perhaps the world had worn him down as well?

The cabin had no power. Here, he read and wrote by the light of propane lanterns fed by copper piping that also fueled a cook stove. In the fall, when the cabin turned from a fishing place to a bird hunting mecca, the oven produced a remarkable apple pie. But this time of year, thick sliced bacon from the general store eighteen miles away, fried in a cast iron pan, dominated his senses.

Firestone's only responsibility today was to decide where to fish. Heat emanated from a woodstove and took the spring chill from the air. As the day promised to warm, he let the fire dwindle and set out for the Big Hole.

A half-mile walk along a deer run, the river made a "Z" set of curves, and in the pocket of the second bend, untold years of current had scratched out a deep hole where brook trout hid in the shade. He fought his way the last few yards through the tag alders that lined the river below the ridge. Opposite the Big Hole, a sand spit provided a perfect angle to cast above the depression and let the stream carry a fly beneath the far, overhanging bank.

Firestone liked to make his first cast of the year in this spot. He remembered from many years, both good and bad, that he had one chance to nail a keeper brookie for dinner. Every year, one large fish dominated this stretch of the stream, having grown unmolested, perhaps caught and released the previous year. Many small brook trout lived nearby, but only one survived natural selection to feed in the Big Hole.

He laid out a cast and heard a deer splash across the river a few hundred yards downstream. The sound momentarily distracted his concentration, but he turned back quickly at the tightening of his line. He gathered with his left hand while using his right thumb and forefinger to gauge the speed of his winding and to hold the line taut.

Back at the cabin, Firestone cleaned the fourteen-inch brook trout on the picnic table that sat on a high bank overlooking the river. He tossed the guts and head down the bank for the otters and birds. He set the cleaned fish on a paper plate in a cooler on the porch and lit another smoke. The trout would make a fine main course, sautéed in left-over bacon grease.

He had the rest of the afternoon to figure out how to complement the meal.

Cedar Swing

A gentle wind rocked the swing in a cadence like a conductor might twirl a baton for an orchestra to follow. Angelique sensed the wind like Samuel talked to animals. If she told anyone else, they would call her crazy.

Samuel made her crazy. They weren't really related. She belonged to her mother, Marie, Firestone's housekeeper. She kept no memories of her father, though Papa Firestone watched over her like his own child. Her mother called her Angelique, an island French name. Samuel, who liked the way the letters danced in the sky, smiled when he whispered "Angelique" out loud. Papa always called her Angel.

Angel had her own room on the ground floor. The back porch had been enclosed with windows on three sides and extended into the back yard. A worn picket fence separated the cared for lawn from a slope of long grasses that led down toward the clear, flowing creek where Samuel fished. As he always made certain to isolate himself from neighbors, Firestone eschewed curtains that blocked his view of the world.

Samuel's desk sat in an alcove of his attic room, his shadow visible to the outside through a dormer-style picture window. Angelique lay naked in the darkness of her flannel sheets and studied Samuel working by a single lamp. She watched and waited until he turned off the light. A natural tease, often Angel then switched on her bedside lamp, rose, and walked to the window.

Angelique was awakened in the predawn twilight by a rustle she heard through an open window. She sat up in bed. She heard the squeak of the iron gate opening, and in the mist, made out Samuel's shape wearing hip boots as he carried a fly rod down a mowed path toward the creek. A newly born fawn spooked out of the long grass bordering the path and ran awkwardly on gangly legs before stopping to turn and look at Samuel. Samuel stopped, too. He stared into the spotted fawn's eyes. Angelique heard Samuel call softly, reassuring the baby deer, like a mother might coo her child. The innocent fawn listened and turned his head askew for a moment before Samuel tired of the nonverbal conversation. The deer bounded away.

Angelique lost sight of Samuel in the green, June woods but remained sitting up in her bed. She watched as the morning sun broke over the eastern hillside and the earth came alive.

A bluebird perched on a stick protruding from the round opening in a bright green, hand-thrown, pottery house.

The two-person cedar swing began to rock in the windless morning as if she and Samuel rocked together, a vision too good to last.

A yellow, Tiger Swallowtail butterfly floated close to a bush near the window and rested on a white flower before rising away like a balloon, higher and higher, in no particular direction.

THUNDERSTORM

A few days later, Samuel woke to a flash that pierced the panes of his bedroom window glass. Bomb-like thunder followed before he could count two one-thousands. The lightning strike had been almost vertical. In his half sleep, the yellow-orange outline of a notched dagger cut through the dark northern sky.

The late spring morning came peacefully, as it always seems to come following a thunderstorm. He knew thunder and lightning had a special way of waking the earth, of opening paths in rich, brown soil so that roots could dive deep. For the past few evenings, he had listened to the melodious sound of a bird echo from the forest edge. He heard the sound again as he lay in bed.

Up and out of his bed, Samuel headed outdoors with a purpose on this moist, humid morning. Mushrooms and wild leek undoubtedly waited in the wild grasses down the lane. Usually, both the cat and Charlie accompanied Samuel on his walk. Today just the yellow cat followed, leaving the songbirds alone to feed in peace.

Samuel walked the woods, determined to discover the source of the uplifting song. He whistled and received a reply. Perhaps the call was one of the brilliant orioles that sucked orange slices hung from a feeder outside his father's window? A bright red cardinal had also visited, but the red bird preferred ground feeding on sunflower seeds knocked loose by chickadees and brilliant gold finches. Blue jays bullied their way about the yard. One had chased the male cardinal away yesterday, but the squawking jay might yet get his comeuppance. Bullies often miss the muddy, yellow cat who lurks silent and still beneath the snowball bush.

Marie viewed the storm differently. As she prepared breakfast, she searched for a thought that lingered from the uneasy night. Bacon began smoking in the cast iron pan, and flustered for a moment, she was pulled back to her duties. *Marie never let things burn.* She quickly laid the slightly overdone strips on paper towel to soak up the grease. Several snaps burnt her hand. She grasped for meaning in the hot pain, afraid she might discover the message.

A cardinal flew to a perch outside the open kitchen window and whistled a happy tune.

Samuel entered through the back door, leaving wet grass footprints on the plank floor. His pockets bulged with the morning harvest.

His faced beamed as he reached for a bowl, emptied his pockets, and covered the mushrooms to soak in fresh water from the sink. Samuel rinsed his hands, dried them on the towel that hung at Marie's waist, and grabbed two slices of bacon from the counter.

"You get back out and clean those shoes, young man." Marie scolded him halfheartedly, while pretending to snap at his bottom with the towel.

Angelique chose that moment to amble down the stairs. "Snap him good, Mama."

Samuel smiled, craving the attention of both women, and let the wooden screen door slam shut.

"Show-off," Angelique scolded.

Angelique found a mug, poured a touch of cream in the bottom, and filled the cup with coffee from the tin pot on the stove.

She lazed back on a wooden chair, "Some storm last night, huh?"

The telephone clanged nearly off the wall, an intrusion startling both mother and daughter. As the ringing entered a second round, they heard a wail from out near the vineyard.

Marie jumped to answer the telephone, knowing she would hear Old Marge's voice, knowing the news, knowing in her heart that Hector had travelled to the spirit world. Alone at the cottage, he had been clearing brush from the wood pile.

"Water moccasin," Marge mumbled into the receiver.

The bright red cardinal perched on the kitchen windowsill.

Angelique had hurried out the door to find the source of the wail. She found Samuel slumped over a brownish-yellow shape beneath the pinkish-red buds of Catawba grapes. During the night, Charlie had chosen to lay beneath the vines for his final sleep.

Several blue swallows left their nest-building in the barn rafters to swoop like dive bombers for bugs emerging with the warming sun. Angelique pulled Samuel from his knees and held him in her arms. The muddy yellow tomcat cried for attention and rubbed against their entwined legs.

Angelique helped Samuel carry Charlie to a corner of the pasture. They buried him under a flowering chokecherry tree and marked the grave with fieldstones. A lone Sandhill crane croaked, approaching from over the red pines at the top of the ravine, choosing that moment to glide a mere twenty feet above their heads. They craned their necks and without a word, watched in awe as the magnificent bird soared in an arc and returned from whence he came.

Both Samuel and Angelique somehow knew their lives would never again be as simple.

REVELATION

Firestone checked in later that afternoon by pay phone from the general store in Little Lake. He arrived home in the evening to prepare for the trip south to the Georgia islands. He felt the strain of the world's business, foremost to take proper care of Hector.

Marie clutched Firestone as he climbed down from his truck, "Hold me tight," her body said.

Samuel and Angelique stood on the porch, arm in arm, weary from the wait and the unavoidable thoughts that death brings to us all.

"I need a shower and a few hours of sleep," Firestone announced. "We'll leave at dawn. But first, we have some things to talk about."

Firestone loved returning home to the farm just as he loved getting away to the cabin on the Escanaba River. He knew he was lucky to have the best of the world at his fingertips. He often needed his time alone on the river, in the wild where life hung in the balance of everyday decisions, like keeping a fire alive in the wood stove. Should he carry his hatchet or bear spray on a walk in the deep woods? Yesterday evening, before life had taken another turn, he sat quietly in a cedar Adirondack chair on a high bank and studied the peace of the river. A lone mallard flew like a bullet, low, following the course of the meander, landing somewhere downstream. A small herd of deer had watched him from the far bank, wondering, before springing away in a world momentarily without worry.

But the farm gave Firestone a different peace. The first hummingbird of the year. The deep green following the first rain. The buds beginning to show on the lilacs. His family, warm and waiting. Perhaps having lost Sally so young had hardened him to death. He would miss Hector but found himself unable to weep.

Samuel had a fire going in the woodstove to take off the evening chill. He and Angelique huddled together on the leather sofa. Marie passed out four of Sally's pottery cups while Firestone popped the cork on a bottle of last fall's vintage. He poured a healthy dose in each cup.

Firestone began, "Time to set aside my silly pride and tell you all, to tell my son, about his mother. She was a lovely creature, perhaps too good for this world."

Into the darkening night he wove the story of their chance meeting while climbing Bear Butte. He told of following Sally to Spearfish Creek, unwilling to let their chance meeting go unresolved. He knew they belonged together, despite his perception of the world, so young and innocent.

"Without knowing, I had been drawn to a conduit, to the place the Cheyenne believe is the center of the world."

"Oh Papa, Sally. You met Sally on Bear Butte," Angel exclaimed.

Firestone went to the bookshelf and retrieved an original two-volume set, *Sweet Medicine* by Peter J. Powell. "These books relate the story of a Cheyenne prophet, Sweet Medicine, who, in the early 1800's received a sign from the Great Spirit during a yearlong fast in a cave on Bear Butte, called Noavosse, the Good Mountain."

"I've read the story, father," Samuel replied. "I've read many of your books."

In the morning, the family set to packing the *Woody* as an experienced crew sets a vessel ready to sail. Firestone favored substantial vehicles, and the Jeep Wagoneer would carry the family safely south. Angel had the most to pack, as she would be staying in the St. Simon's cottage until the term began at the Art Academy in Savannah.

Once on the road, Firestone continued his tale as the family listened, raptured. He looked at his son in wonder, in a new light, realizing that he was no longer a boy.

"Later, I discovered that Bear Butte was formed by a volcano that never erupted."

"Someday, I want to travel out west, like you did Papa," Angelique announced.

With me, I hope, Samuel thought.

Marie studied the young pair, the way they looked at each other, the way they communicated without words.

"How did you find Sally?"

As they drove south, Firestone continued his story, and the miles flew by as he spoke. He told of a waitress in Spearfish who knew Sally and of her mother's reluctance to accept their relationship at first. He had to return to his grandfather's farm in Michigan to help with the fall harvest, ever knowing that he would return out west at his first opportunity. He left out the intimate details , but his feelings were apparent to his listeners.

The long day's driving had tired the family. Firestone's sudden revelation, along with Hector's passing strained their senses, and the rush to try to do something about death tired their minds. The effort naturally proved futile. Samuel shared the driving, and when his eyes began to tire, Firestone suggested they stop for the night near Lexington, Kentucky.

"Let's get some sleep, regain our wits, and drive through to Georgia in the morning."

Firestone and Samuel shared one room, while the women settled in another. Before showering, Firestone set his things on the dresser: his wallet, a pocket flashlight, and the bone handled knife that he always carried. Samuel lit the bedside lamp, knowing that his father always read a chapter in whatever book he had with him to relax before sleeping, a trait Samuel had copied.

Firestone lay down and found his bookmarked place. He was working through Ambrose's *Undaunted Courage* for the third time. He wondered at the wisdom of the adventurers, who several times split up the party. Somehow, they always met back up at some out of the way corner of unknown wilderness.

He set the book aside, now alone with his son. "I know you would like to stay down at the ocean, sail, and swim, and spend time with Angel, but your education must come first. And you know as well as I that northern schools will better prepare and challenge you."

"I know father, but those places are all so stuffy. Rich, privileged kids, I won't fit in."

Firestone believed in the merits of a public education. He knew from experience that a young man should work while studying; learn to earn his own way. He had seen the effects of wealthy families pampering their children, children who never grew up.

"You can play ball and fish in your spare time. Maybe spend holidays in the Islands."

Samuel knew his father was right, but accepting the fact depressed him. Finishing prep school at the farm would be fine, but college, all those years away from nature, away from Angelique? He closed his eyes, rolled over, and fell asleep.

In the morning, Angel rode up front and sat entranced, unable to take her eyes away from this father figure whom she thought she had known. Firestone took the back roads through Smoky Mountain National Park and suggested they stop for a picnic lunch by a mountain stream.

Firestone sensed that someday, with their entwined spirits, Samuel might have the good fortune of traveling with Angel. A casual observer might mistake the pair for brother and sister, but Firestone knew better.

"Tell us more, Papa. I want to know more."

They packed up the picnic, fought through traffic near Asheville, and worked their way through South Carolina. Firestone pushed on, and they talked into the summer evening. He wanted to see his beloved ocean before dark.

"After the harvest, I started west, full of myself and in love like a buck in the rut. On the way, I stopped and camped for a night overlooking the Grand Canyon. I found a certain peace looking out at the magnificence of creation. I had great plans to sweep Samuel's mother off her feet, get married, and live happily ever after. The next day, December 8th, 1941, I learned of the Japanese bombing of Pearl Harbor."

Spirits come to us in many different shapes and forms.

Wake

Old Marge and Emily had cleaned the cottage, put on fresh sheets, and greeted the family, each in turn, with squeezing hugs. Marge had even covered her shrimp smell with the penetrating odor of Irish Spring.

A nervous energy filled the room, the feeling of not knowing what to do with one's hands.

Angel began, "Charlie died yesterday morning, too. I helped Samuel bury him back up north."

"I am so happy y'all have come home," Marge blubbered. "Hector would be pleased having us all together."

Firestone replied in his usual firm and wise voice, "We can only stay a short while. Samuel has school back in Michigan. But family is important in times like these. Dealing with Hector's passing becomes our collective burden to bear."

"In my mind," Marie added, "that old goat still stands outside with a shovel in hand like the day he took me and Angelique in back on Cumberland Island."

"Me, too," Samuel adds, "I'll always see Hector waiting for me after school, me and Charlie. He always made time to talk while he worked, put up with my silly questions."

"Aye, he had a certain wisdom born of hard work," Firestone replied. "He knew that the only silly question is the one never asked."

Angel and Samuel made the trip to Cumberland with Old Marge, Emily, and Sheriff Callahan, who drove the group to the ferry landing. Marie and Firestone had gone ahead to pick up the urn.

"He seems callous," Angel murmured, "so calm, like death doesn't matter."

Old Marge met the Sheriff's eyes as he spoke, "When you have seen the suffering that Firestone has, you learn to set it aside. You believe in a better place, or death will ruin you."

"Papa will not talk about the war," Angel replied.

"Yes, please tell us, Sheriff," Samuel asked.

"War changes a man," the Sheriff began, "Sometimes for better as well as for worse. War embodies no reason, makes no sense. Only the strong-minded can survive some memories."

Joe Callaghan had served in the European theatre. He and Firestone had occasionally shared snippets of their stories to each other after too many rums on the porch. Talking about the war came hard, especially to those who could never really understand. But Joe saw the yearning in Samuel's young eyes, the need to understand his father. He told them what he knew, what he had pasted together over their years of friendship.

"Your father became a Corpsman, an unsung hero. He saved lives rather than take them. He served in both theatres; Italy and the Pacific Islands."

Old Marge hugged Angel like a daughter and wiped the tears from her eyes. Samuel gained a certain pride in his father that he had never known before.

Samuel and Angelique walked down the brow of the ferry to an old wooden dock. Firestone and Marie waved from the beach. Family and friends strolled slow yet purposefully through the sandy paths that led to the ocean side. They passed the ruins of an old homestead and stopped to watch gentle waves break over the broad shore.

In an intimate gathering on Cumberland Island, Firestone tossed Hector's ashes to the wind. A few wild ponies looked on in curiosity at the diverse group. Some of Hector's friends from the old days had made the ferry ride from the mainland on a windy summer day. Only Firestone noticed Camille's lonely figure watching from a distance. She stood cloaked beneath Spanish moss that draped from an ancient live oak.

"Dry those tears." Firestone smiled at Angel in the Jeep on the way home. "Hector is in a better place."

"It's not Hector. The Sheriff told us stories about the war, at least what he knew. I cannot imagine the horror."

Firestone stared out the windshield at the broad expanse of St. Andrews Sound. The tide gurgled in. The same tide that had carried Marie and Angel to Cumberland Island. The same flood that had washed Samuel up on the beach after Hurricane Harriet.

Conflicted, he pulled the truck off the road onto a sandy, prominent point and turned off the engine. He saw Sally in the white peaks of ocean surf. He saw her in the rocky shoreline near San Luis Obispo.

He gave up the fight and finished his story while Angel, Samuel, and Marie listened. Firestone's eyes moistened as he remembered the good times after the war: traveling with Sally along Route 66 and seeing the Grand Canyon on the return to the family farm, the struggles as a young married couple just starting out, finding and building their home and life in the northern highlands, and their chance meeting with George Blackwood, the wealthy industrialist from Memphis.

"Well, I took the man's offer," Firestone explained while coming out of the fog of memories. "And Blackwood had friends, both here in the islands and Up North. They all paid well."

"The sketches," Angel remembered, "those pretty ones that hang on the wall in the cabin in Michigan."

"Sally never saw St. Simon's Island. A trip we never did take together."

Don't put things off until tomorrow.

CHAPTER SEVEN:
1971

Free Spirit

Angelique arrived Up North with a flourish. She had driven through the night from Savannah in her sporty but well-used, light-blue Mustang convertible. Her short, summer-print dress hung loose around her shoulders as she slipped sandals onto her dusty bare feet before running up the path to the porch where Marie waited for a hug.

Samuel couldn't help himself. He wanted to act cool and mature, but his excitement moved him to jump up from the kitchen table and rush to the door. Still holding Marie, Angelique opened her eyes and smiled mischievously over her mother's shoulder, "Well, look what we have here."

Marie felt the loosening of Angel's arms and turned to see Samuel standing in the doorway. He beamed with a strange combination of wonder and excitement. Marie knew the look well, from personal experience. She looked at Firestone the same way. Samuel had grown over the past three years and stood tall and tanned from physical labor. Between college terms, he worked long hours outdoors unloading boxcars full of white pine lumber from Canada, and when he wasn't working or playing baseball, like his father, he spent his free time alone on the river. Marie watched; there was no mistaking the depth of the embrace between Samuel and Angelique.

"So, where did the car come from?" Marie inquired suspiciously. "I thought you were going to take the train?"

"Oh, I bought it from a man down on the wharf. Actually, I worked the price off dancing, nights after school. Burns oil and tends to over-heat, so I try not to drive in the hot sun."

Angelique set her portfolio case down on the oak, country kitchen table. With a sense of drama, she lifted out a charcoal sketch.

"Oh," Marie exclaimed, "this is the St. Simon's cottage. The porch, and the live oak, such detail."

She carefully lifted another charcoal drawing, Samuel sailing *Wanderer* with St. Simon's Sound in the background, and Charlie perched on the bow, nose to the wind.

"From memory, for you, Samuel."

"I'll build a frame today," Samuel exclaimed, "and we can hang good old Charlie up in my room."

"Not so fast, mister, I have another."

She reached into her case and carefully pulled out a watercolor, depicting a similar scene, except that Angelique had painted herself into the picture, riding the bow, while Charlie sat alert in the cockpit with Samuel.

"This one is for the whole family," Marie decided. "Firestone will love it. Let's find a spot above the mantle and surprise him."

Restless Days

Samuel had anxiously awaited Angelique's arrival up north. Though he could talk to his father and Marie, he could truly confide in Angelique. She would understand his need for a change, a new direction, a new challenge. College classes seemed irrelevant. He had lost his all-American drive and questioned his faith in the system. Samuel saw the hypocrisy rampant in Lansing and Washington. He saw the nightly news, the body bags returning from Southeast Asia like so many fallen dominoes.

Baseball had always given Samuel an outlet for his feelings, a place in his heart without questions. His promise had been beyond dispute before politics enjoined the game. He began to show up to his semi-pro Flyers' games tired from long hours at the lumber yard. Coach Geyser had never favored Samuel because he had done well in "school ball." Geyser coached with a negativity born of the street and played psychological games with Samuel's head. Baseball was no longer fun.

Firestone's worry grew daily. After hearing of the Kent State killings, Samuel had quit the college baseball team and hitchhiked to Washington D.C. for a peace rally. And now, he sensed Samuel's lack of interest in summer ball. Firestone had seldom missed a game.

He wondered if Samuel had also lost his drive toward law school. Firestone knew the boy had inherited his father's independent streak. He beamed with pride at Samuel's good sense, but Firestone had been lucky in life. Fortune favors those who work hard and leave the complaining to others. Samuel never shied away from hard work. And he had such a utopian passion for an essential fairness among men, for the tenets of the Declaration of Independence. Yet Firestone still worried for his son's future. His concern increased algebraically with Angel's return to Michigan.

Angelique watched out the window while Samuel filled the feeder with sunflower seeds. A goldfinch hovered close and nearly landed on Samuel's shoulder. She watched him gaze at a bright bluebird perched on the top of the sundial. She became the bluebird, the focus of Samuel's attention.

The night before, during their lovemaking, she felt his neediness, his vulnerability, and his underlying strength. She knew she should tread carefully with Samuel's feelings, yet she loved him so completely, she was unable to hold back. How quickly his virile confidence turned to quiet introspection.

Samuel swung the screen door open and washed his hands at the kitchen sink. The suet he had put out for the pileated woodpecker covered his hands. He felt trapped by the grease and hurried to scrub the feeling off, like scraping a bug from the windshield.

He turned to see Angelique watching and blurted, "I need to get away."

"I know," she replied.

She had Samuel on a string, but the string was bound to her wrist, and to her heart. "I promised to meet some friends from downstate next week. We're going to a concert in Toronto, *The Moody Blues*, my old roommate got tickets a month ago."

"Just girlfriends?"

"Jealous, silly?"

"Maybe. I thought you didn't get along with Julia?"

"I know, but I promised. When I get back, we can take a trip, see someplace new. Gather together as much cash as you can."

PARTING SHOT

Samuel turned toward the outfield and took a deep breath. He tucked his MacGregor glove under his arm and rubbed the hardball down with both hands. Strands of growing blond hair flowed from beneath his cap in a slight June breeze. With the count at three and one, he turned toward the plate and smiled like the Cheshire Cat at the batter, Bobby Mortons, an old High School teammate, a mouthy rival.

Semi-pro ball, top of the ninth, two outs, score tied at one, man on second, and Mortons hitting cleanup for the Legion. Mortons stepped out of the box and glared out to the mound, "Wipe that smile off your face, Sammy-boy."

Coach Geyser stared from the dugout. Samuel had been his last option to pitch the ninth after the star starter pulled up lame after eight. Samuel had loved his high school and college coaches. They understood his sensitivity. Samuel learned young that some coaches teach and nurture, while others challenge. Geyser, a constant challenger, had always threatened Samuel with the bench.

His next pitch came a little too close to the middle of the plate but dropped just a fraction of an inch. Morton fouled it off. Count, three and two.

Samuel smiled again, oozing confidence. Don't overthrow, relax, natural motion.

His best fastball of the evening nipped the outside corner, low in the zone, leaving Mortons flatfooted as the umpire raised his right fist, "Strike three."

Samuel loosened up in the on-deck circle. His whole world watched from the bleachers. Marie and Firestone, who never missed a game, watched but Samuel didn't notice. He gazed at Angelique who stared back and studied this young man who had been a boy when she last saw him. Now a college man destined for a great future.

Samuel watched his teammate strike out on four pitches to a tough lefty who would soon be signed to a minor league contract with the Erie Seawolves.

Samuel took the first pitch, a strike on the inside corner he knew he couldn't reach. The lefty tried the same pitch again but missed inside. Somehow, Samuel knew the next pitch would be a roundhouse curve that would start high outside the strike zone but drop and paint the black edge of the plate. He stepped out of the box, took a deep breath, smiled, and stepped back in.

He never felt the contact as the ball hit the bat.

Samuel started hard out of the box, easing up halfway to first base to watch the high fly ball sail above the 340-foot marker in right center field.

He smiled as he touched the plate with Angelique looking on with pride.

"I knew you could do it," Geyser spouted, obviously trying to get back in Samuels' good graces. "Our new closer. You waited on that curve just like I taught you."

Samuel kept his thoughts to himself.

The next morning, Samuel and Angelique packed for a swim and a picnic out on the McSauba beach dunes. "Before you leave for Toronto, we'll stop by Geyser's place on the way. Gonna' drop off my Flyers uniform for good."

COUGAR DREAMS

Samuel broiled inside. He worked extra shifts at the lumber yard and saved every dollar. Unable to sleep, he read constantly. He discovered a new bookstore in town. A young couple, up from Ann Arbor, opened the store. Beatniks, he figured, his hair long and braided, hers cut close like a man's. They took books in on trade, so when he finished Thoreau's *Walden*, he traded for *Utopia* by Thomas More. He ran through two Dickens' novels in one sitting. When he finished those, the man handed him a thin book of veiled poetry, *Trout Fishing in America* by Richard Brautigan. That one, he kept.

She had left for Toronto with her girlfriends. When would Angelique return? Would she return?

Exhausted after four days, Samuel finally slept, falling into a deep dream, a dream he hoped to remember once he woke up.

In a cave on the face of a cliff, a cougar strides with purpose, paces with underpowered steps, and waits for an opportunity to pounce.

Her cat's gaze fails to reveal intent. She never betrays her thoughts.

Samuel sees a moving shadow. He feels a presence and quickens his pace along the rocky path that follows the ravine at the base of an almost vertical wall. Dark, irregular holes dot the dusty surface. Colorful ribbons in the rock, worn and reformed and worn again by time provide hundreds of places to hide. He takes a moment to stop and wonder; has fear caused him to exaggerate?

The shape moves again, but he cannot pinpoint the cave. His eyes deceive him. He trusts nothing. He wonders if he could stroke the cougar like a barn kitten, who shares her shape and movement, but not her muscular, elongated body. Given the right setting and mood, perhaps he could make the cougar purr.

He finds a rock outcrop that overlooks a small spring and sits to await the waning, forty-five-degree light that will illuminate and calm the desert. The creatures who live near this place will come to drink. All beings need water.

In his haste to walk, he has forgotten tobacco, so he gathers a few sage leaves, rolls them together in a tight bundle, and lights the end. The smoke alleviates his desire and rests his nerves. He has made his offering and will trust the maker of all things to protect him from the cougar.

With eyes closed, Samuel's senses awakened. He relished the restful peace of unmeasured time between wakefulness and sleep, safe in soft, flannel sheets. Outside the window he heard the muddy yellow cat purr. He wrapped his arms around the covers and drew them close to his face. Samuel dwelled in the moment, someplace between dreams and daylight.

CROSSING OVER

Angelique's better sense told her to go home, to blow off these jokers. She wanted to be back with Samuel, to run away and explore the Black Hills, to see the west, like in Papa Firestone's stories.

Julia had roomed with Angel at Miss Marianne's for one term before being expelled from the Savannah School of Art. Her mother's second marriage had been to a wealthy auto executive from Grosse Pointe, a shirttail relative of the Ford family. Julia had no talent for painting, just money, and a wild need to push the limits of reckless living.

Angel had vivid memories from a trip on mescaline the evening that Julia had moved in. *Flashbacks*, she heard them called, from her first and only experiment. Angel had wandered through the park across from the boarding house and reveled at the surreal images, the way the dew hung on the leaves. She had finally fallen asleep on a bench beneath a live oak tree and dreamed of capturing the image on canvas. But she awoke unsettled.

Julia brought other drugs into her life, ones she vowed to avoid. Like nearly everyone in her generation, Angel had enjoyed smoking a bit of pot. Even straight old Samuel smoked a joint from time to time. But Julia carried speed, and cocaine, a rich kid's scourge. Often strung out for days, Julia would finally crash and sleep through a day or two, missing classes. Angel worried for Julia, felt sorry for her, really, for the way she wasted her opportunity.

Angel pulled the Mustang though an iron gate into a circular drive that led to an expansive brick colonial. Julia ran out of the front door carrying only a flowered cotton bag and jumped into the front seat.

"You'll have to drive; Daddy won't let me take the car."

Julia's mother looked on from the porch in disdain at the white, burnt oil smoking out of the Mustang's exhaust.

Julia had invited friends, a pair of rich boys from Grosse Pointe. More than friends, Angel surmised by the way Julia teased. And what had Julia promised them? Apparently, Angel was only there to provide a ride.

Why did I agree to come?

She felt Rollin's shifty eyes constantly staring as she shifted the stick on the Mustang. He studied the way her faded sundress inched up her olive-colored legs and occasionally offered a glimpse of her panties. Julia and Marcus lay beneath a blanket in the back seat.

They ran into a bit of a hassle at the border crossing in Sarnia. Angel's Georgia license had expired, and when the agent asked her birthplace, she stuttered while lying, "Cuh, Cumberland Island."

"Your license was issued in Savannah, Georgia."

Angel recovered her composure. "I go to school in Savannah, but my father lives up north, near Petoskey, Michigan."

"And you two, not avoiding the draft are you?" The agent smiled, after checking their ID's. "Go on through."

For a few hours during the concert, Angel forgot her worries. She had hurried down the gradual grassy embankment toward the natural amphitheater in the park. She danced alone, swaying to the music, and believing the message of "The Days of Future Passed," if only for the moment.

When the music ended, she worked her way back up through the crowd to find her passengers and be on her way home. She looked up at the falsely lit sky of the city, and experienced Déjà vu. She saw a feral female cat, beige, probably a cougar, who lived alone by her wits in a rocky landscape. The sleek, muscular cat appeared from a cave on a ridge overlooking a pond formed by a trickle creek. The cougar poised to leap upon an unsuspecting fawn.

Julia had run into more acquaintances from Grosse Point. She and Marcus had dropped blotter acid and lay sprawled on a blanket. Julia, nearly incoherent, "Oh darling, we don't need a ride. We'll stay the weekend here."

Angel sighed, relieved to be rid of Julia, and strode silently toward her car. Rollin, panting, caught up to Angel when she reached the Mustang parked three blocks away. Angel cringed when he threw his knapsack in the back and got in. They drove in silence. Angel worried about the rising thermostat on the dash. She worried more about how she could get rid of this leech.

Rollin gawked through his evil eyes and reached his hand toward her thigh. Angel let loose of the wheel with her right arm and caught him just below his left eye.

"Damn," he cried, "I get the message."

Rollin picked up the road map. "We better take the highway toward Windsor up here a few miles."

"Why," Angel asked, "I want to drop you off. I need to get home."

"I picked up a cheap pound of grass back there in the park. We should probably cross into Detroit. You had enough trouble getting through in Sarnia with nothing on us."

Furious, Angelique found herself unable to think clearly. She wanted to ditch Rollin right there, in the middle of Ontario farm country. His long, black hair hung unkempt and covered one eye.

"You had no right," she yelled across the too close space.

The line of cars entering the United States at Detroit from Windsor reached a quarter mile back on the Ambassador Bridge. They watched as every third or fourth car was directed to the side, torn apart, and searched. The Mustang inched closer to the gate. The thermostat climbed.

"Give me the dope," Angel said. She tucked the thick plastic bag down her jeans.

"Your car is overheating, Miss," the agent said as she pulled up to the gate. "Where were you born?"

A Traveling Home

Firestone had gone to the cabin up on the Escanaba River to catch the last of the early summer fishing before the black flies hit. He wanted Samuel to go along. The boy's mind seemed tied up in knots. Some time on the stream might have relieved the pressure cooker of a young man's yearning, but Samuel had a bad case of young love.

Samuel knew that the engine block on Angelique's Mustang was cracked. He envisioned a long slow drive across the prairie, through the badlands and into the Black Hills, and wanted solid transportation for the trip.

Samuel walked through the yard. The yellow cat tagged along. He heard the warning cries of songbirds who knew the cat prowled. A bright green hummingbird hovered a few feet from Samuel's head near the glass tube filled with sweet water. Safe from the cat, six feet above the ground, the bird looked Samuel in the eye, seemingly finding trust.

Crab grass had begun to overtake the garden. Green leads grew from a deep central root, spread like a spider's web and enveloped hills of summer squash and zucchini. Samuel's sense of order demanded that he pick up the pronged hoe. As he dug one root, he found another, and realized that weeds had no end. Sweat soaked his shirt.

The yellow cat rolled on his back and cried for attention. Samuel reached down and rubbed the cat's belly, but quickly withdrew his hand before playful claws caught the meat of his fingers.

A teapot whistled with steam. He picked an early golden cherry tomato, rubbed the dirt on his pant leg, placed the plump fruit in his mouth, and bit down whole. Simple pleasure exploded his senses. He felt peace here and struggled to understand his desire to travel.

"Beautiful," Marie exclaimed when Samuel unrolled the waist of his shirt and laid two golden globes on the counter.

Marie wiped the dirt from one tomato on her apron and bit down. She filled a glass with ice and fresh mint sun-tea and set it down in front of Samuel who had picked up the morning paper and studied the classified ads.

They had told neither Marie nor Firestone. They told no one about their plans to travel. Samuel hardly believed himself, but he had given final notice at the lumber yard.

Samuel lapsed into thoughts of his cougar dream. Most times, he didn't remember dreams right away, but they might return to him at odd moments. He believed dreams predicted the future.

Marie saw the worry in Samuel's eyes, "What's on your mind, young man?"

"Oh, a dream. I was in the desert being watched by a mountain lion. I woke to that old Muddy cat purring outside my window."

Marie trusted the dream world, but she was careful with conclusions. She sensed that they were losing Samuel to his restlessness. He sought something out of his grasp, some trail he had to follow.

"She should be home soon, that wild spirit," Marie laughed, "but you never know what direction the wind will blow her."

Samuel returned his gaze to the newspaper.

"What are you looking for?"

A few hours later, Samuel pulled into the gravel drive in a beige Volkswagen Bus. The four speed had given him some trouble. He was used to his father's automatic transmission and had missed second gear twice, screeching before he figured out the tall, loose shifter. The engine ran smoothly but strained when he floored the gas pedal to discover the limits of his new van.

Marie stood on the porch and shook her head. Samuel set about washing the van, inside and out. Over the next day and night, he removed the back seat and built a wooden cabinet and bench along the driver's side to hold a propane stove above a bent, tin ice box. He sanded and finished a table in front of the bench, and in the far back, formed a platform to hold a double mattress. He installed curtain rods over the windows and one that separated the front bucket seats from the rear living area.

"Marie, do you have some bright material to sew curtains?"

"Where are you planning to go, young man?"

"Angelique and I are going to get away, a summer vacation. Maybe climb Bear Butte, where my father met my mother."

Marie cringed when he told her, though she already knew. She couldn't stop them. Nor could Firestone, but there would be hell to pay when Papa returned home.

Angelique called late that evening. Her car had broken down on a country road in the Thumb. A county sheriff stopped to check. He smelled marijuana.

"Trouble, Mama. I need cash. Ask Samuel. They impounded my Mustang. I need money for bail."

Flight Risk

Marie hurried to her bedroom and reached for the King James bible propped on a shelf next to a photograph of the family before a Christmastime dinner back on St. Simon's Island. Sheriff Callaghan had one arm around Hector, the other around Ellie. Marie and Firestone hovered behind Samuel and Angelique like guardian angels. Everyone smiled.

Marie had cut out a section of Revelation, a chapter that scared her, the one that the Baptist preacher way back on Cumberland Island told her never to read. She pulled her life savings from the bible and handed a thick roll of hundred-dollar bills to Samuel.

"You take that girl to safety," she told Samuel, "away from here. She will die in that podunk jail."

In Bay City, Samuel guided his VW camper over the Saginaw River Bridge. He avoided the freeway where crazy tourists drove much too fast for his liking. Once out of the city, he worked his way south and east along square country roads that never varied from the four cardinal points of the compass. He slowed for a tractor pulling a wobbly hay wagon and watched as a sunburned farmer paid him while taking a wide turn into a farmyard.

Pickup trucks roared by, passing him like moonshiners at high speed. He smelled their exhaust and wondered how the pollution affected the rows and rows of dark green corn beginning to grow between shelter belts of tangled trees and bushes spaced neatly into forty-acre fields. A pheasant flew closely by his windshield. The bird's bright, red neck startled Samuel from a daydream. *Lucky*, he thought, *those trucks would have smashed the bird.*

In the quiet farm town of Sandusky, husky women going about their shopping stopped and stared at the funny looking, foreign van puttering down Michigan Highway 46. Near the town square, a muscular farm boy got out of one of the trucks that had left Samuel in the dust. His bumper sticker read, *America, Love It or Leave It.*

Samuel parked diagonally on the square near the courthouse. A police car pulled in next to the farmer, who waited for his buddy, a young deputy sheriff, to get out before yelling, "Get a job, hippie."

The county judge had wasted no time. Angelique had been arraigned at nine a.m. He set her bail at five hundred dollars, figuring a half-breed hippie would never come up with the money.

"Angelique," he asked with disdain, "what kind of name is that?'

Angel bristled. "French," she replied, "any educated person would know that."

Despite muted protest from her court appointed attorney, the judge set a trial date for the first week of August. Let her cool off in the county jail for a month.

"I need a bath," Angelique said later that afternoon as she and Samuel walked down the courthouse steps. "Let's find a lake and take a swim."

CRYSTAL LAKE

Samuel pulled into a gas station in the small town of Clare. Angelique, who had been resting in the back of the van, woke, "Do you have some dimes? I'm going to call Mama, let her know I'm alright."

"Sure, let her know we're heading west, and we love them."

Samuel finished cleaning the windows on the van. Angelique, looking concerned, ambled across the lot and climbed into the front passenger seat.

"Mama says hi and be careful. She also said you got a letter from the government. She opened it. You've lost your student deferment."

Samuel turned his head into the west wind. A snowy white cumulus cloud floated like a ship against the azure sky.

"Oh Samuel, they're going to draft you. You know they'll send you to Vietnam."

"Well, I guess we're both on the run now."

During the three-hour ride across lower Michigan, Angelique slept with her head against the window. Samuel just wanted to put miles between them and the troubling thoughts running through his head.

Keep moving on down the road.

Sparkling afternoon sunlight shimmered on wind ripples over the expansive lake as they descended the highway that had been built on an ancient sand dune.

Samuel reached over and gently shook Angelique's thigh, "Here's the lake."

He drove along the north shore. Summer cottages, hidden behind old growth trees, overlooked the lake. He turned through overhanging vines down a grassy two-track that opened upon a simple, shuttered log cabin. From the cobwebs and lilacs taking over the windows and the unkempt weed-grass lawn, he figured some old folks had passed on some time ago. *An unwanted summer place.*

A spotted fawn munched on hosta leaves. The young deer looked up when Angelique hopped from the van and only reluctantly bound into the woods on spindly legs.

Angelique tossed off her sandals and ran down a sandy path toward the lake. Samuel followed and stooped to pick up her shorts from one bush and her blouse from another. He heard the splash before slender popple trees opened onto a narrow patch of beach. He tossed a bar of soap into the lake, "Catch."

Angelique dove for the ivory soap, unaware that the white cake would float. Breaking the surface like a porpoise, and seeing the ivory floating on the surface, she called out, "Brat."

Samuel laughed and stripped off his jeans and tee shirt. He walked slowly, letting the clean white sand bury between his toes. To the west, he noticed how an enormous sand mountain damned the cold, spring-fed lake. The dune separated the crystal-clear water from *the Big Lake*, Lake Michigan, an inland sea. Summer, yet the water iced his legs.

"Only one way to do this," he yelled, before diving headfirst, breaking glass into rippled sun-shards.

They bathed and rinsed and frolicked until goose bumps began to appear on Angelique's arms. Samuel collected pine branches and started a fire in a fieldstone lined pit where a charred chunk of log remained unburned from the last blaze. He strung a line between two maple saplings to hang lake-washed clothes to dry. Marie had packed some things for Angelique, and she knelt bronze and beautiful tending the fire in a yellow sundress.

Samuel stood and gently lifted the light cotton from Angelique's shoulders, and they lay entwined on a quilt before glowing embers, two gentle souls hidden from the world.

Dream River

Darkness surrounded two shapes kneeling by a campfire. Overhanging maple leaves cast changing shadows. At an out of the way local market, Angelique had insisted on a string of homemade sausages filled with cheddar cheese, two of which were suspended over the fire. Creamy goodness melded with the sizzling pork and satisfied their burning hunger. Samuel popped the cork on a bottle of his father's sweet wine.

"In the morning," Samuel suggested, "I thought we might take the car ferry across the lake to Wisconsin."

Wide awake with anticipation, Samuel ran on about the ferry to Wisconsin and where they might go next, "We'll see the mighty Mississippi River, and decide from there. Maybe the Black Hills, Bear Butte?"

Angelique, exhausted from the day's stress, made her way to the van, "Tomorrow, tomorrow."

Samuel poured a second helping of wine into a tin cup, leaned back against a maple trunk, and studied the outline of her sleek body as she collapsed on the mattress. Soon, his chin dropped against his chest, and he drifted into dream sleep.

Alone in gathering darkness, Samuel dreamed he neared the end of a long day's journey. He scrambled up the side of an abandoned railroad grade. Upon reaching the top of the cinder and gravel surface, he stood and looked out across the bubbling current of a deep, dark river.

Past the crumbling concrete trestles on the far side, lights twinkled through the windows of shops and taverns. *One more river to cross this day*, he thought, *and a tricky one at that.*

In the dream, he surveyed the near shore from the height of the rail bed and perhaps thirty feet below and a quarter mile to the east, a two-track road ended at a boat landing. Out in the river, an old man in the rear of a long canoe skillfully played the current and guided a dented aluminum craft toward four cedar posts anchored in bottom mud that marked a makeshift dock.

A wild-haired young girl stood in the weeds near the landing. Her face was hidden. She waved at the old man in the canoe.

Samuel stepped down the grade, stumbled, and slid, almost surfing in the loose stone. He regained his footing in the long grasses near the river shore, began to trot, and reached the sandy spit on the land side of the dock just in time to grasp the bow of the canoe and pull the man and the boat up on shore.

The old man, somehow familiar, stretched his long legs over the side of the canoe, his boots splashed through shallow water, and he offered his strong, weathered hand, "I've come to retrieve my daughter."

"Might you have room for a passenger? I'd be happy to pay," Samuel replied.

The old man stared at Samuel as if reading his mind. "Hop in, son. Daylight wanes."

The girl sat down in the canoe bottom between the two webbed seats. Samuel led the bow around into the current, tossed his leather knapsack to the girl, stepped in, and settled on the forward seat. The man splashed through the shallows, pushed off the bank, jumped in the rear, and barely avoided soaking his feet above the top of his boots, "Grab that paddle."

Samuel pulled hard, changing sides, while the old man steered into the strong current. "We'll paddle upstream past that near trestle, then let 'er glide across."

Samuel felt a welcome ache in his shoulders and turned to the work at hand. He hardly noticed a blue heron standing like a statue on one leg in the grass. A beaver slid into the stream carrying a willow branch in his teeth.

After several minutes paddling against the current, the man called out, "I've got it from here." Deftly, the old man placed his wooden paddle in the steaming dark water.

Samuel enjoyed the downstream ride. He reached out to let his fingers glide across the rough, concrete surface of the near trestle, but as he was dreaming, felt nothing. The canoe cut across the main stream, riding on the crest of the flow toward the far trestle and the dim lights of a town.

As they grew nearer, Samuel made out the village landing though the moonless night. Adjoining the far trestle, an old dam-like structure led the river away from the mainstream, bifurcating the current into a narrow passage between high seawalls on both sides. The landing lay on an eddy backwater just beyond the tunneled river.

As the old man began to guide the canoe into the entry, a strong gust of wind shifted the stern downstream beneath a rippling wave. The powerful current dragged the stern ever downward. The canoe flipped and submerged.

Samuel struggled, swimming for the surface to gasp for air. He felt his body bobbing along through the tunnel, and clearing water from his eyes, watched the canoe disappear into the deep. The man splashed frantically and called out, "My daughter."

Treading water, Samuel searched for any sign of movement. Time froze as he focused upon oil-like swirls patterned on the surface. Through the dark depths, myriad worlds took shape like friendly ghosts. The face in the photograph of his mother smiled down. A hand touched his forehead. Marie stared from the familiar porch in St. Simons, waiting and worrying. She called out to Samuel, bring her Angel home.

An arm broke the surface twenty yards downstream. Samuel swam hard, pulling with his chest muscles. He remembered racing as a young boy, freestyle, the backstroke and the butterfly, and thanked the heavens that he knew how to swim.

The girl's head bobbed. Samuel reached for her arm, which had become entangled in a line from the canoe. Treading with only his legs, Samuel unsnapped the sheath on his belt, and with the sharp bone-handled knife Firestone had given him, sliced the line free. The girl struggled and screamed for her father. Samuel gathered her arms together, flipped her over, and with gentle force, took her surprisingly light weight in tow.

The old man stood by the edge of the landing where slimy rock riprapping bordered the river. Samuel strained to pass the now calm girl to the old man, to safety. Hanging from the wild-haired girl's opposite shoulder, Samuel felt the leather strap of his knapsack. As he let her go, he reached for his knapsack that held his memories. He reached, and then she was gone.

Suddenly alone in his dream, Samuel struggled to climb up the jagged, slippery surface before slipping back into the water.

A pack of coyotes howled in celebration of a kill.

Samuel startled awake near embers of the dying fire. River currents flashed through his mind. He remembered the dream. He had slipped back into a watery abyss.

Unable to reconcile the real world with his dream, he frantically stumbled to the van, and tucked in beside the warmth of a sleeping girl.

A Silent Crossing

A ray of sunlight glared through the van window. Samuel reached up to pull the curtain shut. Still groggy, he realized he was alone.

In the shallow sand of the lake, Angelique lifted a bare leg above the waterline and soaped her ankle, shin, and thigh. She scrubbed her groin and repeated the operation on the other leg before lowering into the water to rinse. Samuel watched from the van and grew restless watching.

An uncomfortable distance clouded the air between the driver and passenger seat as Samuel drove the van onto the USS Badger, a car ferry that ran sixty miles across Lake Michigan, from Ludington to Manitowoc, Wisconsin. Samuel parked the van in the bowels of the steel-plated behemoth. As they ascended the stairs to the main deck, Samuel touched Angelique's arm to guide her toward the tubular arm rail. She pulled away and lightly bound up, two steps at a time. His heart dropped in his chest, and he followed slowly.

Across the faceless crowd, he spied her standing at the bow, her hair ruffled by the wind. "What's wrong?" he asked.

"Nothing, just tired, I guess."

Angel did not understand how she felt. Confused, certainly. Afraid, a bit. Thoughts ran through her mind like a freight train about to hop the tracks. She loved the boy so deeply, and until now, so selfishly. His intelligence and understanding knew no bounds. He had unlimited promise that would remain unfulfilled if he became a father so young. She could only hinder his future, but she knew how Samuel adored her, and how the hurt of letting him go might also ruin her.

Samuel unscrewed the cap from his green Coleman thermos, poured the cap half-full, and handed the creamed coffee to Angelique.

"Bear Butte," Angelique volunteered, "that's where Papa met your mother. Let's climb Bear Butte."

He drove the van across the gang plank into the neat, little town of Manitowoc, where square streets were lined with solid brick buildings. *German craftsmanship*, he thought, while smoothly shifting the VW van into third gear.

"We'll take our time," she said while studying a map, "back roads, see the countryside. Turn here on Highway 21. That will go west across Wisconsin. Then we'll cut north to Highway 8 to cross the Mississippi River."

Old Man River

They drove through the rich farmland of Wisconsin where dairy cows grazed peacefully on deep green grass. Samuel pulled over at a farm stand at the end of a driveway that led to a neatly kept white house. An oversized American flag was painted on the barn for all to see. In an adjacent field, a farmer on a green John Deere tractor pulled a hay rake and turned over the previous days' cuttings.

A robust woman in a flowered dress and apron stayed out of the sun beneath the makeshift roadside hut. She looked askance at the young pair of travelers, "You're not from around here, are ya'?"

"No," Samuel replied. "Just passing through. We're headed west. We'll take a brick of that baby Swiss cheese. Is the bread fresh?"

"Baked this morning," she said pointedly, and handed the paper package to Samuel, whose blond hair had begun to grow long, and his beard several days removed from a shave.

"My boy is fighting for our country over in Vietnam. An even five dollars should cover it."

Samuel felt guilty. He had been privileged, protected by his success in school, by his father's wealth. Now, out on his own, a runaway, potential felon, he had turned his back on some innate social responsibility that gnawed at his soul. Angelique might not understand, think him silly and naïve. He kept his thoughts to himself.

Dusk settled as Samuel pulled the van around a wooden barricade and into an abandoned park along the St. Croix River. Angelique slept soundly in the back.

Samuel quietly opened the door and got out to stretch. He walked to the river's edge. He sat down and rested his back against the mottled white and brown-grey of a sycamore tree. He heard a rustling in nearby bushes and watched an otter slide down the bank into the stream.

A red-tailed hawk ascended from his perch on a tree stump and swooped in search of prey.

Samuel closed his eyes, and soon, as in a motion picture, saw himself handing a jug of water to an old man with a knapsack who rested on the tree stump where the hawk had perched. The old man's eyes were familiar, simultaneously soft and penetrating. His wrinkled visage welcoming.

The old man pulled a Swiss army knife from his pocket and whittled a point onto a long sycamore branch. Curled white cuttings littered the ground around his boots as the point grew sharper.

"Quiet now," the old man whispered, and stood erect as a rabbit eased his twitching nose from beneath a wild blackberry bush. The old man poised to strike.

A single coyote yipped upriver. Soon, a howling chorus echoed through the dark night. Twinkling stars, and the steady glow of Jupiter seemed so very close. Samuel reached out to touch the heavens. He turned toward the tree stump where a red-tailed hawk perched absolutely still. He fell asleep.

Samuel awoke to the shriek of a red-winged blackbird. A lone, female wood duck traded down the St. Croix River, heading south. A strange feeling overwhelmed him as he hurried up the path through the sycamore trees. He reached the van.

Angelique was gone.

Chapter Eight:
Samuel's Journey
1971

On His Own

Inked words floated like boats along the sea of lined paper. Samuel studied the words over and over but found himself unable to make sense of the message. His stomach ached. His eyes blurred.

"You will be better off without me…"

He looked around the van. The emptiness echoed the queasiness in his gut. Feminine things were no longer tossed about. He opened the glove box and found the envelope from Marie opened. A few bills remained from the thick wad of cash he had never counted. His dreams fell apart, shattered like shards of glass from a broken vessel.

And his knife, his old Swiss Army knife in a form-fitting leather case, also missing. He touched the bone handle in the sheath on his belt and felt some reassurance.

Samuel walked to the river, spread his arms out like wings, and screamed to the high branches of the sycamore trees. The prehistoric, guttural sound caused several crows, a pair of mallards, and a mourning dove to take flight in unison and answer him, each in their own tongue.

In the coin pocket of his Levis, he felt for the smooth, round Petoskey stone that they had found along the beach back home. He rubbed the surface before violently pulling the rock out. He reached back to pitch the offending mineral into the river, out, far out into dark waters, forever.

The abrupt halting of motion hurt the muscles in his throwing arm. A vee of Sandill cranes croaked overhead. Samuel watched as they glided across the river while he kneaded the smooth stone surface.

Perhaps I'll wait a bit.

Samuel started a fire in the pit, noticing the ashes left over from the night before. When the coals glowed, he fried three strips of thick bacon in the number eight cast iron pan, added two fresh eggs, quickly flipped them over, and made a sandwich on wheat-grained bread. He returned to the river, sat on a stump, and watched for signs of fish rising as the sun cleared the morning mist.

A circular dimple appeared from the depths, first one then another. Breakfast finished, he walked back to the van, strung his fly rod, and tied on an Adams pattern fly. He pulled on his hip boots and returned to the stump. Though he knew he shouldn't, he lit a Camel cigarette to keep the small but irritating black flies away from his face. He felt the rush of the smoke hit his brain, and when he stubbed the butt on a stone, felt the pressure of the smoke in his athlete's lungs.

After a few false casts, Samuel laid the fly out on the end of an eddy and a fish hit before the fly settled into the water. The fish rose into the air and pulled. He gathered in the line, and landed a lovely, slender, brown trout.

This will make a fine dinner.

Samuel camped by the St. Croix River for two more days and nights hoping against reason that Angelique might return. On the fourth morning, he steered the van west over the bridge spanning the river.

"Alright then," Samuel firmly stated, out loud, "On my own now, heading west."

His heart carried a loneliness deeply buried in a cavern that never sees the light of the sun.

Samuel drove through the day following two lane country roads across Minnesota. West of St. Paul, he stopped for gas. One pump stood high on a concrete pedestal that stuck out of the gravel drive. A flying horse adorned a glowing, glass sign mounted upon a green steel tower.

The attendant strode out of the station. Samuel rolled down his window to the deep voice of Jim Morrison blaring, "Break on through to the other side."

"Fill her up. I'll check the oil," Samuel yelled over the music.

The attendant's long, greasy hair hung over his eyes while he washed the bugs from the windshield.

"Four-twenty for the gas," the attendant said, "ninety cents for the quart of oil, and we have a deal on sunglasses, if you're interested."

Samuel counted out five, one-dollar bills and eight quarters. "Thanks, keep the change."

The attendant and the station disappeared in the dust of his rear-view mirror.

Near dusk, Samuel came upon another roadside park on the east shore of the Red River. He sat near the water and snacked from a bag of loose granola that Angelique had left in the cupboard. A pair of mallards, the bright, green-necked male and the homemaker-brown female glided to rest in a backwater pool.

Such a perfect pair, mated, peaceful, and happy.

Samuel parked the van near the bank where he could watch the birds as sunset calmed the day. On the far side of the river, a gaggle of Canadian geese flew back and forth, searching for a safe place to land.

Samuel Sees the Mountain

Samuel crossed the Missouri River near Forest City and entered the Cheyenne River Indian Reservation. Shocks worn to nubbins, the van bounced with each irregularity on the rough blacktop road. His mind rattled too, bumping between rolling hills and thoughts of the girl he loved without pause, no matter how things had been left unsaid.

Endless, empty prairie and rolling brown hills broken by rock crags helped to soothe his mind. He passed a native tending sheep, no house in sight. Fierce and solitary hawks hunted from fence posts. The land seemed to float like the Atlantic Ocean, where in childhood he sailed *Wanderer* and where he had first met Angelique. Samuel became lost in the splendor covering the high prairie. He faded into a land of reverie until awakened by a darkening western horizon.

A mammoth shape approached from the southwest. A rapturous cloud rolled in the sky and charged toward him like a puffy, white stallion. In the distance, lightning outlined the lonely shape of a mountain. Thunder clapped, harmonizing with his cassette tape of Dvorak's *New World Symphony*. A concert and light show resounded above the shadowy Black Hills. Samuel's navigator sense kicked in, and he knew while some forty miles away that his path would cross the solitary shape, *a natural wonder*, Bear Butte.

In the dusty town of Newell, he pulled over on the gravel shoulder to check his tires. A sheriff's car stopped in a lot across the road. The officer stared at the van. Beneath a wide brimmed hat, his eyes inspected Samuel up and down before he turned away, apparently satisfied. Samuel let out a deep breath.

The road bent south toward Sturgis. A sign read, *Bear Butte, 20 Miles*. As Samuel drew closer, overcome by an overwhelming presence, goose bumps ran up and down his arms and legs. He reached the base of the mountain shape at the precise moment the sun settled below the prairie. A full moon rose in the east and framed the top of the Good Mountain.

He braked hard, drawn to an unreality, to the almost animated image. The wheel turned in his hand and the van tires skidded on the gravel of the narrow shoulder. A cowboy driving a Dodge pickup adorned by good buddy lights roared by. His horn blared a warning.

Oblivious to the fray, Samuel stepped to the center of the highway and snapped a photograph, catching the moon above the fading red butte. He timed his run back across the highway, dodged another truck, and jumped into the van.

A mile or so up the blacktop, he turned off on a dirt two track and parked next to a narrow creek that ran through an oasis of basswood trees. As if jolted by lightning, he felt a revelation:

There are places in this world where a great spirit has touched the earth. Listen quietly, and God will speak to you.

In the morning, I will climb the mountain.

THE CLIMB BEGINS

"Bear Butte, …where Papa Firestone met your mother," Angelique had repeated over and over.

Mother. Words on a page. Empty promise. Samuel had fortified himself against the thought. He avoided close contact. He would never let himself be hugged, never give in to a desire for maternal care. Who needed a mother? Samuel had done just fine without one.

The tip of his walking stick caught in a crack between sharp rocks. A scrape, the first blemish on the walnut staff he had whittled and sanded while waiting for Angelique. He adjusted his Detroit Tiger ball cap. Cheap sunglasses shifted on his brow. *You get what you pay for*, he chuckled to himself, *and these cost forty-nine cents*. He thought about the attendant at a gas station back in Minnesota.

Mickey's mother had hugged him, before Big Mic killed her in a drunken foray. She held him warmly, snugly, not like Angelique. *What a mother must feel like*, Samuel guessed. And Old Marge, though more of a grandmother, and she smelled like shrimp.

He sensed that this mountain wanted to take those feelings away, to let worry ride on the wind into the endless prairie and become lost in vast infinity, wherever thoughts go. Forgiveness welled up inside him.

Forgive and be forgiven.

He reached a rough-sawn pine pavilion where the gentle slope joined the steeper base of the Butte. A woman with long, grey hair played a wooden flute. A soft sound echoed above the treetops like a preamble hymn calling the congregation to worship. She smiled and waved.

Samuel saw himself walking up the broad steps to a cathedral, like the one he had visited in Provence after his sophomore year in college. *Chartres, perhaps? Certainly not Notre Dame. No river here, no city streets.* He stared up at rock spires where trees no longer grew and stepped boldly forward, upward, to see what he might discover.

FLOATING

A Monarch butterfly rested on wild grapevines.

How did these wild grapes get here? Samuel's mind began to wander. He envisioned a way:

Years ago, another pilgrim must have perched on this rock by the side of the path, chewed grapes, tossed the stem aside, and spit out a seed. Or a bird carried the seed from a distant ranch where a woman tended a few concord vines in her garden. She made jam each autumn. Her husband, a cattle rancher, died last winter, but she still makes jam. Their son moved to the city years ago to escape the loneliness of the prairie. She will have trouble hanging on to the ranch much longer. Eventually, she will escape, too, and spend her days in a small-town retirement home, single-story, like a revamped motel. She will dream of the days on the ranch when she tended her grapevines.

Samuel paused to give thanks for his father. Firestone admired his vines. He passed his gentle vintner's touch down to his son.

If allowed, every vine grows differently. This wild vine took the path of least resistance. Untended, unbothered, undisciplined, a vine grows where it will. Like Angelique.

The monarch fluttered close to Samuel's eyes, turned up the path, and beckoned Samuel to follow.

Quiet now, except for the wind, Samuel turned briefly. In the valley below, the woman with long grey hair packed up her wooden flute. He stared at the colorful contrast, the green and gold grasses, the Black Hills in the distance. He turned again, stared upward toward a defined profile, a face protruding from a rock outcropping hundreds of feet above.

Like the shroud of Turin, or one of those statues that weep. An apparition?

Alone, he was drawn to step forward, to climb, somehow knowing that an answer awaits above.

The Summit

Samuel loomed above the universe. In this moment, from his perch on the summit of Bear Butte, he knew he had reached the highest place on the earth.

Nothing can hurt me here.

He fought his pride, which, as the Bible says, *Goeth before a fall.* With part laugh and part sigh, he realized that he chose venerable Bible verses at a whim. But he knew his feeling of immortality did not stem from pride, not this time.

A mountain blue bird whistled from a nearby rocky perch.

Samuel listened closely to an inner voice. The bird has come for a reason, carries some seed of wisdom meant only for him. Overwhelmed by a peaceful confidence, he pushed bad thoughts away and released his mind to the west wind.

A red-tailed hawk soared above and circled on the upward draft of the mountain in search of prey.

Life is too short to waste, too precious to dwell on the past.

Samuel bound into a determined descent.

Stunned

Samuel turned south at the town of Spearfish and followed a two-lane road along a clear mountain stream. He stopped near an old generating dam that had fallen into disrepair. Chipped concrete held the last vestige of a chain link fence that hung over a pool on the higher, upstream side. Below the dam, a spurt of white water rushed from beneath the concrete abutment.

He watched rainbow trout leap in earnest to scale the height. Out of place out of the water, the silver torpedoes jumped higher with each effort. Finally, a single fish leapt, and with raw abandon, flew over the dam.

A dirt path led downstream to a natural widening. Samuel fought back dense vegetation along the creek, and extending his right leg, jumped toward a boulder. Catching a second boulder with his left foot, he regained his balance. He studied the riffles of the white water and spotted a dark pool on the far bank. He drew a deep breath and released the air purposely from his lungs while he cast a lure toward the eddy.

Almost before the spinner hit the water, Samuel felt the weight pulling against him. A steelhead leapt in a glorious circle, like a trapeze acrobat holding the bar in his teeth. With a little give and take, Samuel loosened the drag before tightening.

He smiled at his thoughtlessness; *Of course I left the net hanging in the back of the van.*

This fish is too heavy for my line, but if I play the tension just right, I might be able to guide dinner to a spit of sand.

Samuel let the steelhead run out hard one last time. Just before the last few coils of line left the reel, the fish turned. Rather than forcing, Samuel guided the streaking trout toward the spit while reeling in slack. At the last possible moment, he jerked the fish onto the shallow sand.

Samuel splashed into the creek, wetting his moccasins and his jeans to the knee, pulling the trout to higher ground. With his bone-handled knife, he deftly cut and cleaned two large filets and wrapped them in fresh popple leaves. Returning the guts and head and bones to the creek, he washed his hands in the cold, clear water. As he climbed the path to the van, he looked back to see another trout rise and devour a floating heart.

A few miles upstream of the dam, he turned onto a steep, two-track mining trail that led up into the mountain heights above Spearfish Canyon. Even in first gear, the van's engine struggled to ascend the trail. Runoff from a recent rain created deep ruts. Sharp shards of limestone that resisted erosion protruded from the grassy center between the two tracks.

Samuel heard a ping of a stone striking the running board followed by the screeching scrape of rock along the oil pan. He gunned the engine. The van bounced through a deep rut and reached the top of a swale. Momentum kept the van moving over the rise and down toward a trickling creek bed. He gunned the motor once more to ford the six-inch deep water.

The canyon wall rose high on his right and a chasm dropped off to the left. With no place to turn around, he had no choice but to push the tinny van to the limit.

Another boulder, another metallic crack. Samuel gripped the wheel tightly as the van jerked down and to the right.

A ball joint, or perhaps the right front axle. No way to stop on this cliff.

The Volkswagen limped up and over the next rise like a sloth with a broken leg.

The trail opened into a mountain meadow, flat at the bottom then extending up a gentle rise bordered by a stand of Aspen. Samuel urged the van toward a ring of stones, an old fire pit, built at the base of the rise.

Finally, a place to stop and check out the damage.

As Samuel relaxed for a moment, he felt the axle give way. The front bumper dug violently into the earth.

As he was thrown forward into the windshield, the last light of the day glowing golden flashed before his eyes before all light disappeared below the shady depths of the canyon walls.

Chapter Nine:
Angel's Journey
1971

SOUTH TO TEXAS

Angel rested her head against the dark window and feigned sleep while never closing her eyes completely through miles of shadowed countryside. How long since she had seen a yard light? The odor of men's sweat permeated the shag-carpeted faux palace, a converted Chevy work van. The dirty smell annoyed her. She imagined a waft of Samuel's fresh, outdoorsy presence. Snoring emanated from the backseat reminded her of a gaggling goose.

She worried about her choice of rides. When Samuel had fallen asleep down by the river, she had gathered her things and walked over the highway bridge leading into a tiny Minnesota resort town. On the outskirts of the village under the last streetlight, she stuck out her thumb.

The driver had picked her up without waking the man in back. A black, three-day beard covered his face and accented his pale, white features. He pushed his long hair behind his ears and looked Angel over with a hard stare, a wanting stare, one she had seen before. She returned an impassive, knowing smile while tossing her pack on the floor and climbing into the bucket seat.

"Where you headed?" the driver asked. "My name is Donny. That's Ivan snoring in back."

"South, somewhere warm, maybe the Texas barrier islands. Call me Charlie," Angel replied, remembering Samuel's coffee-tinged yellow lab, remembering Samuel's gentle touch.

I don't trust this man. I don't want anyone to know my real name.

"Quite a name for a girl. Well, you're in luck, Charlie, we're heading to Austin."

A two-lane highway followed the Mississippi as they drove through the night. She felt herself travelling along on the current of an impenetrable river. The clouds occasionally gave way to the waxing moon and revealed wave caps lapping in the wind. She had not taken a hit from the joint that Donny offered, and when he pulled over in Iowa, just past the Wisconsin line and spread white powder on a woman's compact mirror, Angel continued to resist. She had an urge to try that stuff, to sniff and become lost, but the night by the fire on Crystal Lake came back clearly in her mind. Angel knew a child had been created, her child, Samuel's child.

Did Samuel know? No, he's just a boy, how could he understand?

"Roust out, Ivan, your turn to drive this buggy."

The shape in back stirred with an evil air. Bearded, and his brown hair combed perfectly to imitate a biblical prophet, he stared directly into Angel's eyes, as if trying to communicate a sense of superiority without words. Angel answered with an unyielding glare. She had seen his kind before.

Donny shook out a sleeping bag and spread it open on the carpet floor. He unzipped his black leather boots and tossed his shirt, along with Angel's pack onto a guitar case. He pulled the suicide door closed and lay down. Angel deftly closed the forward door, and as she began to climb to an empty corner, the van lurched forward. She fell backward. The stranger wrapped his arms around her shoulders, pulling her toward him. Angel kicked out, caught him in the groin with her heel, and curled up in a ball by the window.

"Damn, you're a wild one. I'm too tired anyway. I'll leave you be tonight. Tomorrow is another matter."

Morning came harshly. She felt dirty, wishing for her mother's claw-foot tub back in Michigan, wishing the night had been a dream.

"Arkansas," Donny called out while kneeling by a campfire in a roadside pull-out, "we passed through St. Louis in the night."

A macadam grade led a few hundred yards down toward a ferry landing. Angelique stared in awe as several snapping turtles ambled along the road toward the river in no apparent order. *A migration of sorts*, she thought. Samuel would love to see the green shells etched with shapely, yellow caricatures. He would understand. He would know why the creatures crawled with such purpose.

Ivan walked toward the van, cinching up his belt, having used the primitive, log outhouse across the park. He intentionally cut through a second campsite where an older couple sat at a picnic table enjoying breakfast. The pleasant aroma of bacon frying had Angel's taste buds churning.

Angel enviously studied the couple's silver-bullet-like trailer adorned with stickers from a myriad of travels. Most notably at top, a blue, red, and gold circle was etched with the words, *Semper Fi*. And standing out on the bumper, Angel read, *America – Love It or Leave It*. She hoped Ivan would not antagonize these simple, old folks.

Donny called out, "Hurry up, Ivan, the ferry's coming."

Angel chided Donny as he drove toward the ramp, "Watch out for the turtles."

From the back seat, Ivan called out, "See if you can hit one!"

Donny intentionally turned the wheel. Angel's stomach cringed at the sound of a shell cracking beneath the van's tires. Donny slapped Ivan's hand with a high-five. Angel turned her head to the window in disgust.

A grizzled old man glowered from the side of the ramp. A one-man operation, he guided the cable ferry, raised and lowered the ramp, and organized the parking arrangement on the steel, four-car deck. Angel became distracted when a bluebird perched on top of the wheelhouse. The bird seemed to watch the old man walk toward the van to collect the toll.

Donny pointed toward the passenger side, "You can at least cover the fare."

Angel quickly opened the door and hurried toward the ferryman. With her back turned to the van, Angel handed him the four-dollar fee. A red-tailed hawk perched on an oak limb overhanging the river. Angel read the questioning in the ferryman's eyes.

You do not belong with those men.

As the ferry approached the far shore, Angel returned to the van, beginning to plot her escape. "Hey Charlie, hope there is more where that came from," Donny sneered, looking her up and down for a hiding place.

She settled into the back while Donny and Ivan shared the driving throughout the hot, humid day. Angel listened to their banter of dreaming, how they would meet up with an old buddy who went to school in Austin. "Man, the good times we'll have."

Ivan pulled a gallon of Gallo red table wine from beneath the seat and poured two full mugs, handing one to Donny at the wheel. The pair grew wilder with each sip, and as they passed through Shreveport, Angel's offers to drive were continually rebuked. She laid down in back and prayed. Just before sleep finally arrived, she remembered seeing a green highway sign, *Austin, 40 miles.*

In her fitful dream-state, Angel heard Samuel, alone on a mountain-top, calling her name.

Angel awoke with sweat streaming down her face, her hair matted and stringy. She was alone in the back of the clammy van, parked in a driveway in a ramshackle neighborhood. A threadbare couch sat on the dirt lawn in front of a brick, two-story house.

Once home to a happy family, now worn and weary from neglect.

Two doors down, several small, foreign cars were parked on the lawn of a huge mansion. A battered sign read *ATO* in Greek script. In the dawning light, no one stirred anywhere along the street. She assumed that Donny and Ivan were inside sleeping.

Angel stuffed her clothes in her knapsack. One of those characters, or both, had searched for her cash without success. She quietly stole out the door and hurried down the street toward town. At an intersection, a car came to a stop, Angel heard the radio through an open window; "The Sounds of Silence" wafted softly in the air.

She called out to the woman driving, "Please, can you direct me to the bus station?"

Hustling several blocks, she smelled the diesel exhaust before she saw the station. Once inside, Angel turned and pulled the cash wad from her front jeans pocket and purchased a one-way ticket south.

The announcement couldn't come soon enough, "Now boarding for Corpus Christi, Galveston, and points south,"

Angel stared out the station window trying to make time fly. Finally aboard the Greyhound, she put her pack on the overhead rack. She sank into a reclining bus seat, and with Samuel's sweatshirt for a blanket, slept all the way to Corpus Christi.

SAN PADRE ISLAND

Warm salt water lapped at her ankles. Soft Gulf sand oozed between her toes. She longed to hear Samuel say her name.

She watched the almost fluorescent crabs skitter from hole to hole on the beach. The tide began a slow march toward flood. A trickle current etched a path in the rivulet that ran beneath a bridge from a brackish marsh across the sand-ridden, two-lane blacktop.

Angel liked the looks of the sleepy, resort village the moment she arrived. She had no real plans. After a healthy breakfast at the clean, laid-back *Blue Moon Diner*, she read the handwritten ad on the corkboard by the door. Summer waned toward September, and the help had returned to school for the winter. Josie, the cook, chef, and chief bottle washer hired her immediately. Angel donned an apron before she cleared and washed her own dishes.

On the same cork board, several rentals were available cheap for the off-season. Like the college kids who worked the resort town, the tourists had also returned to their split-levels and their towns and schools and day-to-day winter lives.

Cassie came into the Blue Moon most late mornings for coffee and conversation and quickly noticed the new girl. The whole town would soon. After all, Angel was stunningly beautiful, and she moved so gracefully. Strangers noticed something familiar in her fluid movement, like a wild animal trying to appear tame.

Josie introduced Angel to Cassie, a wealthy real-estate speculator, "Meet Charlie, my new server."

"Charlie? That's odd, what's your real name?"

Angel, tongue tied, longed to tell the truth, but she needed more time to trust these folks.

"Where's your home? You're obviously not from around here," Cassie continued to pry.

Josie, sensing the reluctance in this unusually tanned young woman, intervened, "More customers, Charlie, can you handle that four-top?"

When Angel walked out of earshot, Josie sat down with Cassie. "Seems like a really nice girl, and a hard worker. She needs a place to stay. Don't you have a flat for rent?"

After the lunch rush, Angel walked along the beach following Josie's directions, "About three-quarters of a mile. Painted bright-blue, two stories, on stilts. Can't miss the house."

Cassie waved from the lower porch. "Here you are, Charlie. A hundred and fifty a month. That's off season only. I get twice that a week during Spring Break."

The upper efficiency had a view in all four directions and a small deck overlooking the Gulf. Angel handed her three, one-hundred-dollar bills, "Here's two month's rent to start."

Cassie, who lived in the expansive, lower main house, readily accepted the cash.

Angel fell into the pace of the off-season. She welcomed the routine, the lack of excitement. Most afternoons after work, she sunned on the beach and swam in the Gulf's gentle surf. In the evenings she read on the porch of the upper flat and often fell into troubled sleep on a padded chaise lounge. She was happy when she dreamt. Dreams took her away from her constant self-questioning.

Did I do the right thing in leaving? Could Samuel know? Should I call Mama?

When the racket from Cassie's various night visitors echoed from below, Angel walked the edge of the sand where the surf lapped and the crabs played until the lights dimmed in the main house and she could no longer see Cassie seduce her catch of the night.

Angel recognized the visitors. The men sat together for lunch at the main, long table in the diner. The regulars included a carpenter they called Rowdy; Buck, an electrician's apprentice; and various day laborers whose main tool was a shovel. They dressed in worn leather boots and jeans. Outside work tanned their skin and the sun streaked their unkempt hair. As she delivered the daily special, Angel overheard scraps of conversation while maneuvering to avoid their reach. Whenever Cassie came in, talk became muted, overshadowed by chuckling.

Josie knowingly rolled her eyes. She had been the pretty one in her day, the topic of conversation among an earlier generation. Sand and sun and hard work had taken her sparkle, but her strength remained. The Blue Moon gave the village a meeting place and an excuse to talk to neighbors. Josie presided over her diner like a judge ruled a courtroom.

Angel avoided conversation. She knew the locals wanted to draw her in, especially Rowdy. They watched her like the men back in Savannah. Like most men who didn't bother to look beyond her body.

But never Samuel. With Samuel, her life had been fulfilled and rounded into a full circle.

His touch, she pined for his understanding touch.

Blue Moon Diner

"I know that voice," Angel muttered, startled.

She shook and dropped a fork. She reached down to pick it up, and rising, turned to look through the service window, past the center table where construction workers sat and laughed. Donny, his back turned, questioned Josie.

He pushed his long black hair behind one ear. Josie, animated as always, her arms accentuating each word, nearly hit another customer with a hard, plastic-covered menu.

"No, I said I do not know anyone named Charlie. Would you like a seat?"

Angel watched Donny push open the glass exit door and turn up the street toward a Chevy conversion van. Ivan's familiar shape lingered on the sidewalk. Donny climbed into the driver's seat and Ivan scrambled into the passenger door. With a screech of tires, the van turned north toward Galveston.

"Asshole," Josie commented when she returned to the kitchen. "Rude son of a bitch."

But Josie watched curiously as Charlie carried a metal tray of Melmac plates out to the center table, eggs over easy, thick bacon, and wheat toast. *I'll ask her later*, Josie thought.

Angel saw the concerned look in Josie's eyes, so like her mother's. *Josie knows.*

Cassie sat down at the main table, took a sip of coffee, "What did I miss?"

Angel delivered the plates one at a time and ignored the stares. Rowdy dominated the conversation, loud enough for the whole diner to hear, "Did you see that lowlife? Soft white hands, and those fingernails. Best get his ass back to the city."

A bonfire burned bright against the night sky. The sea breeze sent flecks of light haywire, curling up, ever up into the heavens to compete with constellations. Angel looked on from her upper balcony at the crowd below. She recognized shapes. Rowdy, outlined by the fire, chugged a can of beer.

And Josie's silhouette, the first time Angel has seen her relax among the younger folks. She sat on a log and nursed a bottle, while Buck, kneeling in the sand, bent her ear. Angel could almost see Josie's eyes drooping, tired from a day's work at the Blue Moon and too much cheap, sweet wine.

Cassie swayed back and forth, flirting with the younger men who drank and watched her and hoped they might catch her interest for the night.

Other shapes filtered by. Headlights flashed on the highway. She heard a car door slam and the muffled laughs as partygoers stumbled and fell on the dunes. Hungry for some company, this night of all nights, Angel descended the dark, exterior stairway to the beach. She hesitated, watching a sea turtle lumber into the surf.

"Well, the mysterious one," Cassie called out.

All the men turned their heads. Cassie's luster faded, lost to a new beauty in town.

Josie smiled and handed a tall bottle of Yago sangria to Angel, who sipped lightly, just a taste, and handed the bottle back, whispering, "My real name is Angelique. I am with child."

"I could tell honey. Such a lovely name. Your secret is safe with me. Take your own sweet time. Everything will work out for the best."

Josie took another gulp and returned her attention to Buck, twenty years her younger who apparently had enough of Cassie's continual charade and saw his night warming up against an older woman.

Angel noticed several younger men and a few women she had seen at the diner occasionally. Some paired off and wandered to the dunes, only to return minutes later. The spent young men gawked at Cassie, and furtively slipped a look over at Angel, quietly illuminated at the far edge of firelight.

Behind Angel, on a small dune, Rowdy sat alone facing the sea. Through the shadows, unpredictable flashes of light illuminated his features. His back profile presented a godlike appearance.

Angel ambled over, "What do you see?"

Rowdy looked into her eyes and hesitated. Slow, she discerned, deeper than he lets on.

Angel extended her arm out beneath Rowdy's chin. "Jupiter," she announced, "A friend taught me that stars flicker, but planets glow in a steady light."

Rowdy craned his neck as Angel said, "Good Night," and walked up the beach to the stairs.

Jupiter, Samuel's favorite planet, his good luck charm.

Angelique, coffee cup in hand, wrapped only in a cotton blanket, looked out the window at the gentle, Gulf surf and imagined Samuel lying in her bed.

Her hand runs gently over his chest hair.

Running late for work, her stomach grumbled, and a feeling of nausea overcame her day dreaming. In turn, Angelique opened several blades on Samuel's red, Swiss Army knife. She admired the design, including a blade shaped for sawing, two different sized cutting knives, and a corkscrew. She closed each implement carefully. Finally, she reached for the phone.

"Oh my baby, so good to hear your voice. Papa Firestone and I have been worried to a fright. Are you alright?"

"Fine Mama, fine. I'm working at a diner in a beach town down in Texas. Have you heard from Samuel?"

"No. Samuel must be still traveling, out west somewhere. Another letter has come, from the government, the Selective Service. He's been drafted. Please come home."

"But I jumped my bail."

"Don't worry, Papa Firestone has taken care of your charges in Sandusky. There's a hurricane blowing down there in the Gulf of Mexico."

"There's more, Mama. I'm so sorry for ruining everything. Papa will be furious. I'm carrying Samuel's child."

"Oh my sweet girl, Papa will be beyond happy. He loves you both so much, and he dearly desires a grandchild. We will come for you. Stay safe from the storm."

The chance of weather stirred up fear and exhilaration throughout the village. With early October in the rearview mirror and a tropical storm building out in the still-warm Gulf waters, nerves began to show.

A familiar Chevy van pulled into a diagonal space in plain view of the restaurant. Donny pushed open the door like a cowboy entering the Long Branch Saloon. Angel stared him down and turned on her heels toward the kitchen.

Donny grabbed her arm and pinched her firm behind a little too hard, "Come here you tease."

Rowdy quickly got to his feet, yanked Donny around by his shoulder, and threw a punch at the young punk, catching him on his bearded chin. The force of the blow knocked the long-haired stranger into Josie who landed on the next table and rolled into Buck's lap. Buck gently helped her up, then grabbed Donny by his belt and shoulder, and with Rowdy holding the door, tossed him out to the street.

Ivan had the van's motor running, anticipating their planned escape with Angel and her cash in tow. He jumped out of the driver's side and feigned a wise look, as if to talk his way out of the mess. He met Buck's eyes and the forefinger at the end of a muscled arm pointing directly at him.

Rowdy, plain and firm for both to hear, said, "Don't come back."

"Wonder what's brought this wave of assholes down here?" Cassie cynically observed while eyeing Angel.

"Must be the hurricane," Buck noted, changing the subject. "Probably want to surf the big ones."

With a nod, Rowdy suggested that Angel stay with Josie, "She will know what to do in the storm."

Angel boldly replied, "I've been through hurricanes before."

The activity along Ocean Avenue heated up with the pending storm's humidity. Under Rowdy's direction, every able-bodied man helped hang plywood over storefront windows. In his one-ton GMC, Buck made the rounds through the village. He made a mental note of friends who planned to stay and watched as others left the island for safety.

Buck ran a test of the portable generator in his truck bed. He connected a cord into the fuse box at the diner. Beneath the cover of shutters, inside the Blue Moon, Josie and Angel filled jugs, coolers, and milk bottles with fresh water. Their eyes strained against the artificial light.

Down at the general store and gas station, locals were given priority to waning supplies of flashlights, batteries, and gasoline. Though most visitors and residents deserted for the mainland, the regulars at the Blue Moon Diner planned to ride out the storm.

Chapter Ten:
Montana
1971-1972

Commune

Sunlight glared through a crack between two loose planks and shone in Samuel's eyes. He tried to sit up, but a sharp pain in the back of his neck caused him to drop back onto a makeshift pillow filled with rough straw and covered with burlap.

A woman of indeterminate age in a faded sundress, leaned over him and caressed his face. Her long, straight hair hung below small, shapely breasts, and in her current position, tickled Samuel's ears.

"Where am I?"

"Safe," the woman replied, "rest now, talk later."

Samuel eased in and out between consciousness and a semi-awakened state. In the blur, he began to remember, *Bear Butte, I climbed Bear Butte. And fishing. And my van, where is my van?*

He had been determined to make good on his own, without crawling back to his father for help, without putting his loved ones in danger. *If they do not know where I am, they will not have to lie to the government, to the Army.*

The Vietnam War is sanctified murder, and by God, I will not kill my fellow man.

Later, perhaps two nights and a day later, Samuel woke with regained strength. He wandered out of the tool shack where he had been sleeping. A bonfire glowed in the center of a clearing surrounded by several outbuildings that circled a stone farmhouse. A cast iron pot hung from a tripod above the coals. A woman sat on a wooden, three-legged stool and stirred with a long wooden spoon. Her dark brown curls dabbled down her shoulders, merged with red Native patterns on her wool jacket, and accented glassy blue eyes that stared beyond Samuel into the sky.

"I wondered when you might stir. I'm Sister Chelsea, please sit. Have a bowl, sweet brown rice with golden raisins."

Samuel held a wooden bowl out to be filled. "Where am I? Where's my van?"

"Sold," Chelsea replied. "Father Branch towed your van to Rapid. Got a good price. The money will provide us with food and essentials for months, like this rice."

A tall, muscled man strode into the firelight, followed too closely by several younger men. He thrust his hand out toward Samuel.

"Call me Branch. Welcome, Brother, and thanks for the fish. We all ate well."

Samuel recoiled from the light. He needed time to think. "My head, I need to sleep," he feigned.

"Okay, brother, rest one more day. Then you'll need to pull your weight."

A sense of imprisonment overcame Samuel as he watched through cracks in the wall. He counted four men other than Branch, boys; really, dirty boys, who fawned over Branch's every move. Each had the same listless, unfocused eyes. Except one, a mean looking fellow, probably Branch's aide-de-camp and enforcer. He stood to the side and watched for any sign of disagreement on the other's faces.

Women came in and out of view. Branch lifted Sister Chelsea from behind, caressed her breasts, and led her away toward the farmhouse. Other girls paired up with a boy. The unchosen women chose each other.

Outside, embers from the bonfire flickered and cooled. Inside, Samuel considered his escape.

"Up and at em," a tug on Samuel's shoulders startled him awake. "I'm the foreman around here, Brother Nathaniel, and you need to earn your keep."

Samuel dressed and followed Nathaniel out of the compound into a stand of old growth pine. They shared a crosscut saw and dropped a forty-footer.

"We'll leave that to dry and split up this other downed wood, and haul and stack it back at the compound. The sisters will gather and cut kindling when they get back."

Nathaniel left Samuel to his chores. He worked hard, figuring to get on Nathaniel's good side and gain his trust. Just as he hauled the last load, Chelsea and another girl strode into the clearing like prostitutes walking into a bar, "Made a killing this morning. Sister Sweet Pea badgered those hick farmers and only had to show a little tit."

Sweet Pea reached into her dress, pulled out a wad, and handed the cash to Nathaniel, who stuck his hand in the same spot, routed around for any hold out, and finished by rubbing Sweet Pea's breasts.

"Later," he said, and stuffed the money in his jeans. "You and me back to work, Sammy boy."

Silently, Samuel matched Nathaniel stroke for stroke as they sawed a dried spruce into manageable lengths. Samuel took up the maul and split several logs into firewood while Nathaniel watched, "You've done this before, I see."

The two men took turns at the maul while the other stacked. Nathaniel began to open up, "Every Saturday morning, the girls work tourists at the Lead Farmer's Market. Father Branch will be happy today."

Frost glistened on every spruce and pine branch as Samuel roused himself from his bunk in the dorm-style room. He stared out a single casement window.

An illusion. The mountain will crack like a mirror if shaken.

Days turned to months, and while Samuel had earned Branch's trust, Brother Nate still watched his every move. Branch had given him a bunk in the stone house. Occasionally Chelsea attempted to seduce him into sharing a bed, but Samuel resisted entrance to that trap. Branch often chided the other young boys for not working as hard as Samuel, and they envied their leader's attention.

Samuel had almost confided with Chelsea, before realizing her glassy eyes never betrayed her inner thoughts. In every spare moment, his thoughts turned to Angelique.

So warm and then so cold. Why? Why did she leave?

A frosty morning had followed a December dumping of heavy, wet snow. Branch forbade a Christmas celebration or worship of anyone or anything that might challenge his power. But on the Winter Solstice, he allowed his *family* a pagan feast. A full menu included two steelhead that Samuel caught while Nate watched. Branch, the provider, poached a young doe with a compound bow; fresh venison tenderloin hung over the fire. The rest of the meat had been cured for jerky to last the winter. Orange sweet potatoes and brown Idaho's were brought up from storage in the cellar. And the last of the sweetcorn from the garden caused Samuel to remember his father's garden back in Michigan.

No one else stirred in the house. Only embers glowed from the woodstove in the kitchen, and the others lay covered in blankets, unwilling to rise after a long night of mushroom-induced visions.

Samuel quietly gathered what he could carry. He slipped into Branch's room and took his bone handled knife and sheath from atop the dresser. Branch had taken his father's knife from the van and worn it on his belt as if to taunt Samuel into submission. And his mother's quilt was also hidden in Branch's room. Samuel formed a poncho from the quilt with safety pins.

A line of winter boots dried by the fire. He tossed them out the door into deep snow where the boots might not be found for days.

Samuel eased the front door closed and strapped on the rudimentary snowshoes he had made from willow branches with deer hide straps. He walked west, away from the first rays of a rising sun. He reached the safety of heavy spruce cover at the edge of the compound and set his course down the mountain.

WINTER THAW

On the west facing slopes of the Black Hills, the terrain worked toward level through ever-gentling slopes. Stands of spruce and pine were broken only by an occasional logging trail. Samuel avoided the paved highway that led toward Wyoming and the Devil's Tower.

As he walked into the setting sun, the lowering elevations precluded the need for his snowshoes. He hiked nearly twenty miles the first day, up and down and up again, but with each rise, the climb was not quite as high as the preceding foothill. In a cascading fashion, he followed his compass west. Samuel picked a campsite in the deep woods. He broke down his snowshoes, saved the leather, and using the willow as kindling, built a fire. He built a lean-to with spruce saplings and branches and prepared a makeshift bed with the colorful quilt his mother had sewn, his only cover.

Shards rose and sparkled in the dark night, carried by an ever-warming, southerly breeze. Samuel watched the embers swirl higher and higher until they burnt out somewhere in the heavens and he could no longer discern them from stars. Was it the same with people?

Was Angelique an ember that burned brightest before disappearing into memory?

Samuel had walked west from the commune, figuring that Branch and Nathaniel would look for him north toward Spearfish or east in Rapid City. *Branch and Nathaniel will surely follow me to protect their kingdom in the hills.*

Samuel had not told anyone he was a fugitive from the draft. Branch couldn't know that Samuel was unable to hold them responsible for stealing his van. He could not go to the authorities.

Though he had only jerky to eat, a clear stream trickled nearby, providing plenty of water. Samuel spent three days and nights hidden in the woods to let things settle down. On the fourth morning, he hiked the final fifteen miles out of the Black Hills and came upon the rounded, sloping prairieland of eastern Wyoming.

Warm, southerly winds brought an almost unnatural January thaw to the high plains. Samuel climbed over a barbed wire fence and followed the line while avoiding browsing beef cattle and a pillar of smoke rising some miles away to the north. *A ranch house hidden by a swale.* He reached the paved highway and continued his trek, walking the gravel shoulder through a vast emptiness.

He learned to shelter himself from the passing traffic, mostly lumber trucks running logs from the Hills or cattle trucks hauling meat to market. The force generated by the bulk of the semis traveling seventy miles an hour over the two lane blacktop road nearly blew him over. After several hours, he reached the crest of a rise, and in the valley ahead, saw the welcoming oval of a red and white *ESSO* sign at the junction where a north spur met the east-west highway.

The proprietor of the Elkhorn Tavern, *Bryan* embroidered on his shirt, did not seem to mind when Samuel asked only for a glass of water. He dropped his pack and used the bathroom to wash his face and brush his teeth. When he came out, three leather-clad bikers had bellied up to the bar. The January thaw brought out all kinds of folks looking to enjoy the unusual warmth.

Bryan set a long-necked bottle of Pabst Blue Ribbon on the bar in front of the bikers, and next to each bottle, he set down a a square, plastic package like a gum wrapper with a monogram of the Elkhorn Tavern. He also tossed one on the table where Samuel milked his water. *Monogrammed condoms!*

One of the bikers turned toward Samuel and stared before tossing down another dollar bill on the counter, "Barkeep, get that boy a beer."

"Fuckin' hippie," growled a bearded, burly one with *Butch* embroidered below his *Outlaw* patch. "Just another mother's son running from the man."

The man who bought the beer walked over to Samuel's table and sat down. His patch read *Vietnam Vets Against the War.* Dark and handsome in a wild sort of way, he looked Samuel up and down, like a drill instructor performing an inspection. Samuel met his eyes without fear.

"Frank," the man said, extending his hand. "Short for Francis Xavier, but my altar boy days are over. We just stopped for a quick beer. Heading back east to Cincinnati, tryin' to take advantage of the winter thaw, beat the snow. Gonna take the north cut up to Sundance, then jump on the interstate. You look like you been rode hard and put away wet."

Samuel wanted no part of east but figured a ride north to Sundance might keep him clear of any pursuers. A half hour later, Frank pulled over before the eastbound entrance ramp to the Interstate Highway. Samuel climbed off the Harley and shook Frank's hand, "Appreciate the ride. Take care."

"I'd head north if I were you, Canada. The Cong would eat you alive, pilgrim."

Samuel watched for a moment, impressed by the roar of the machines heading east down the ramp.

East, settled, civilized. West toward the unknown.

Last Stand

Samuel walked across the viaduct and stuck out his thumb on the west-bound Interstate ramp. He wanted to see the town of Sundance, named after the legendary Kid, but figured he needed to put some miles between himself and Branch's band. He sang as he walked, feeling the fresh breath of a new road,

"Freedom's just another word for nothing left to lose."

Before long, a semi pulled over. The truck filled with someone's household goods was bound for Oregon. The driver, handle of Pole Dancer, talked constantly on the Citizen's Band radio and hooked Samuel up with a ride north to Montana when they stopped at a truck stop in Gillette.

Samuel climbed up into the tanker that smelled of propane. The moniker *Gasman* was painted on the cab door. When the driver stopped to catch some sleep near Lodge Grass, Samuel took his chance to leave. He hopped down onto the gravel shoulder and walked north.

The wind picked up overnight, and Samuel struggled to keep warm with just his quilt poncho. He settled in a stand of trees just off the road, a kind of oasis fed by a shallow, winding river. In the morning, he walked generally north along the river bottom, hoping to find a bend where he might catch a trout. Ice formed along the rocky edges of the stream that ran shallow in January, a cycle of the seasons. Without luck, he gave up and climbed the bank to the highway. A sign read *Little Bighorn National Monument, 1 Mile.*

The January thaw had begun to turn, and just three vehicles filled parking spots nearest the iron entry gate. A truck and a sedan, both dark green, were marked with the National Park Service emblem. A road-worn, club cab Chevy with a camper top sat alone in the corner of the lot. Samuel's curiosity overcame any fear of being discovered. *After all, I'm only a minor fugitive. They're looking eighteen hundred miles away in Northern Michigan.*

The gift shop and museum were closed for the season. *No matter*, he thought, and worked his way up a gentle path toward a statue-like monument on the top of a rise. Particles of snow blew like dust across the trail. Samuel thought of the movie *Exodus*, the part when the fog floated through the city and only the doors marked with lamb's blood were safe.

A cemetery. Samuel felt a shiver. *A graveyard serving as a National Monument.*

An ankle high chain and strategically placed signs kept visitors on the path. He walked slowly and studied each carved stone. A sergeant rested here, a corporal there. Many of the etched granite markers had settled and leaned with the hillside. Near the top of the hill, Samuel stopped to look out at the expanse. Unassuming, like the private who died close by, lay Custer, the glory-seeking architect of this blemish on the earth.

Justice had prevailed.

Samuel's resolve to avoid the Vietnam war grew stronger. *Such a silly way to die, following Generals and Colonels and Majors and Captains who all followed politicians. Line up, shoot, be shot. Both sides believing they are right.*

Markers also honored the Sioux and Cheyenne warriors where they had fallen. He understood why the Lakota and the Cheyenne had died. They fought to protect loved ones, to protect a natural way of life that revered the earth and sky and water. Samuel hoped he would have had their courage.

He wandered back down the trail as if leaving a funereal. "Sobering, isn't it," a woman's voice awakened Samuel from his daydream.

She stood by the camper; her greying hair gathered in a long braid. She wore blue jeans, Wellington boots, and a deer skin coat lined with sheep wool pulled up at the collar. The woman tugged at her work gloves, "Looks like you need a ride, young man. If you're headed north, hop in."

Ranch Hand

Out in the cold Montana morning, snow soaked his leather gloves. He cut the twine binding with his antler-handled knife and tossed loose bales of hay from an oak plank wagon. Sheep waited below. *So needy*, Samuel thought, *like babies baying for a bottle.*

Libby drove slowly along uneven fields dusted by snow and watched out the back window of her pickup, the same way she might have watched Linc, her husband of forty years who had died in the spring. A handsome woman, weather-worn with largish features, yet beautiful in a country way, she had told Samuel her story on the trip north from the Little Bighorn, or Greasy Grass, as the Cheyenne called the battle.

Last year's lambing had gone well, then the shearing, "Linc could shear with the best. He was quick and gentle, and watched on fondly as the fresh, pink-skinned sheep bleated before running back to the flock."

"Too much for his heart," the doctor had told her the next morning, "blockage, no chance."

Their last farm hand quit when Linc died, "By God, I'll not work for a woman."

Libby had found fly-by-night help to get through the summer and haying season, using kids out of school and even the local drunkard, "He worked one day then hit the bottle for the next week."

Neighbors pitched in when they could, but they had their own spreads to work and herds to mind, "These Montana cattlemen never took to sheep, still resent Linc, barely cool in the earth."

She had needed to get away, to clear her head and think. She bought the pickup top camper with some of Linc's insurance money, knowing that the ranch had been paid off years ago. In the gentle days of fall, Libby left the sheep in the care of a cowboy who had drifted in with the wind. "I took off to visit the national parks before the snow fell. Places Linc and I wanted to see, but the sheep always came first."

She wandered south to Yellowstone, of course, to see the geyser spout, then down the Wind River Range of Wyoming. She camped all the way, spending a couple weeks in Rocky Mountain National Park before heading back east to the Black Hills. After watching the buffalo in Custer State Park, Libby had called the ranch to check in as she did a few times a week. But the last two calls, no one answered. "I called the county Sheriff and asked him to run by the ranch."

She waited by the pay phone in a truck stop near Gillette. "No one there, Lisbeth. The cowhand's gone. Good luck though, the warm spell, the sheep have been grazing. That dog is keeping an eye on things, but you best come on home."

Samuel had shown up at the right time.

A gift from God.

Samuel pressed a hot washcloth into his closed eyes, a ritual on mornings when he shaved. The warm water seemed to cleanse his thoughts as much as his face. Each time he washed, he felt fortunate for hot water, yet missed the cold water of the stream back home. Fresh, wild water woke a person up for the day. His thoughts turned to a northern lake and a cold morning bath.

Angelique knelt by a campfire.

Maggie, Libby's Scottish Wolfhound, nuzzled up to his leg, then tugged on the cuff of his Wranglers. He had always been partial to Levis, 501 button downs, but damn, in the bitter winter on a Montana ranch, a zipper worked easier. Anyway, the Farm and Seed Co-op only carried Wranglers.

The large, muscular dog with an always questioning look made Samuel a bit uneasy. Libby had named her Maggie after reading an article in the *National Geographic*. Maggie had a fierce god-like demeanor, watchful, almost doting over Libby's wellbeing. Maggie watched over the sheep. Wolves and coyotes provided no match for her lineage.

Maggie stayed with the sheep even after the cowboy deserted the ranch. With noble and powerful grace the dog met Libby and the truck upon her return home. Maggie took only a moment to decide that the stranger could be trusted. Without fear but slowly, Samuel extended his arm for the dog to sniff.

"Careful young man," Libby warned, "she could take your arm off."

Maggie sniffed Samuel's hand, then briefly glanced toward Libby before returning her gaze to Samuel with her head cocked.

Samuel winked, and Maggie winked back.

Samuel settled into the ranch routine, though he worried about regular visits by the County Sheriff. Sheriff Watson had been a good friend to Linc, and by the look in his eyes, had a bit of a crush on Lisbeth. He called her Lisbeth as only Linc had before. By the way she reacted, Samuel could see Libby resented the familiarity. She had taken Samuel in like a son; in fact, given him her son's room in the house. She rationalized this move by the savings on power and heat in the bunkhouse that had fallen into disrepair. Daniel's name only came up when the Sheriff stopped in for coffee.

"Hell of an athlete," Watson said, "quarterbacked the high school football team, but loved baseball, and took a scholarship to Missoula, where the coach turned him into a pitcher."

Libby looked at Samuel, "Daniel, like so many young people of your generation, lost his faith. He dropped out after two years to find himself, his purpose in life. But when the draft notice came, he answered the call. Both Linc and I tried to get him back in school," she tapered off.

"Might have made the big leagues," the Sheriff added, "but ended up in a humid, hell-hole in Southeast Asia."

Libby pulled on her canvas barn coat and walked out the back door.

"Damn shame, not like my war," Sheriff Watson said, eyeing Samuel. "But a man has to serve his country."

Samuel always retreated to his room without engaging. Though he dearly wanted to explain his point of view, he saw no use. Firestone had served like the Sheriff. But unlike Watson, Samuel's father understood that Vietnam differed from World War II, that the cause was unjust, that patriotism came in varying forms.

Libby spent most evenings listening to music in front of the kitchen woodstove, where she worked on the farm books. She particularly like Dvorak's *New World Symphony* played at high volume on Daniel's Pioneer stereo. Dvorak carried Samuel back to his first visit to Bear Butte. He missed his father and home.

Angelique, aside a campfire, on a blanket near a clear lake.

Samuel took advantage of the sprawling bookshelves that overflowed through every room of the house. The black and white console television hardly ever came on, except on Archie Bunker night, when the two souls shared a laugh. Daniel had amassed a record collection very similar to the records Samuel had left back at the farm in Michigan.

Libby would allow Samuel to play The Moody Blues' *Days of Future Passed* but she balked at Crosby, Stills, Nash, and Young, "Daniel's favorite, I cannot bear to listen."

Some nights when Samuel walked by the hall window he saw images flash outside in the darkness. For a moment, he thought someone was there, outside, watching. Weeks passed before he discovered the flashes were reflections from the mirror on Daniel's medicine cabinet. Samuel opened and closed the cabinet door several times to recreate the images.

Still, I see a ghost.

Days were filled with chores and passed quickly toward spring while nights lingered. Samuel read himself to sleep and hoped to dream of Angelique. He slept well, except when Libby walked the house fretful, and looked through the crack in his bedroom door as she once had to check on Daniel fast asleep.

Samuel had planned to leave in the spring, but the lambs came. Under Libby's tutelage, he learned the art of shearing, and her dependence upon Samuel grew.

A creek ran through the ranch weaving toward the Yellowstone River. When chores left him some energy, Samuel sat on the edge of the stream as he might have back home. He occasionally took a trout on the fly.

"Such a lovely fish," Libby would exclaim, just as Marie might have. "I'll fry some potatoes to go along."

Maggie took to the boy as her own. In the long daylight of summer, Samuel often spent nights in the field with the dog by his side. The Montana sky really was bigger than the rest of the world. The stars came out at night in such splendor, and on a hillock on a ranch near the Canadian border, he sailed the *Adventurer* over blue waters with Angelique riding the bow.

Chapter Eleven:
New Life
1972-1973

After the Hurricane

Marie did not wait for another call from Angel. She sensed trouble. A wavering in the girl's voice lacked Angel's usual nonchalant confidence.

She and Firestone arrived on San Padre Island on the morning in the near aftermath of the storm. The bridge remained closed except for emergency personnel, but Firestone had persuaded a young National Guardsman to let them pass.

They found nothing but rubble at the address Angel had scribbled on the postcard. Seeing the beach house destroyed, "The Blue Moon Diner," Marie thought out loud.

Firestone weaved through debris scattered along the town's main road. A downed power line sparked against an abandoned Dodge. Sand and seaweed covered the pavement. Windows that had not been shuttered from the wind had been shattered by flying debris. Glass lay strewn along the sidewalks and sparkled in an ironic morning sun.

Marie spotted the remains of a sign, *Blue Moon Diner*. A stake truck was parked outside. A generator grumbled in the truck bed. A power cord led into the shuttered building.

Inside, Josie leaned over a makeshift bed formed from two tables wedged together. She recognized Marie right off, the dark skin, her gentle features.

"Careful, a falling beam hit her head. She's with child."

Firestone had served in the Pacific Theatre. A young Navy Corpsman assigned to a Marine unit, he had seen his share of death and danger. He never talked about the Philippines or Iwo Jima or the blood that floated in the warm surf along myriad beaches in places forgotten. But he remembered the skills that had helped him care for wounded soldiers. Some had been favored by triage. Many never came home.

Their Angel lay before them unconscious but breathing smoothly. The gash on her brow would leave a scar. No matter, he thought as Marie supported Angel's head, and he counted, "One, two, three…"

With the help of Rowdy and Buck, they lifted Angel from the table to a makeshift stretcher that Rowdy had cut from a plywood shutter. Josie padded the board with several blankets. They carried her to Firestone's Grand Cherokee wagon and slid the board beneath the raised tailgate.

"No time for goodbyes, just thanks." Marie squeezed Josie's hand. "Thanks for watching over my girl."

"Just a moment," Josie walked to the kitchen. "Here's Angelique's knapsack."

Josie unzipped the pocket on the front of the pack. She handed Marie a red Swiss Army knife and an envelope. Marie fanned the cash like a card dealer and stuck out several bills toward Josie. "This will get you started."

Josie refused the money, "Oh, please, no debts between friends."

"It's only money, *mon ami*; you have given us so much more."

Firestone turned from the door, "Josie, thank you for caring for our Angel. I promise to settle up for your kindness. Looks like you could use an investor to help rebuild."

Rowdy and Buck waved as Firestone and Marie sped off through the devastation, avoiding the downed power poles and other debris. He set a course for Houston and the best care he could find for Angel.

Angel awakened beneath the glaring lights in a Houston hospital. She pulled at the intravenous tube taped to her wrist. Marie had dozed off in a chair by the bed but jumped to her feet with the first movement. She smiled and soothed Angel's face with her hands.

Disoriented, her head pounded, her eyes struggled to focus, but she recognized the warm hands caressing her face and the gentle voice.

"Slow down, little Angel, relax," Marie said.

"Samuel? Where is Samuel?"

Firestone rose from a chair in the corner and hustled to the door, calling out buoyantly, "Doctor, she's awake."

"Rest," the doctor had said. "The baby is fine now. Time will tell."

Angel faded in and out of consciousness. Shadows and light flashed intermittently, sending streaks of pain to her head. Firestone had refitted the Cherokee to create a soft bedroom, and in a dream-like state, they made their way north. The first flakes of December snow, always the largest, most unique shapes, floated by the windshield in the dark.

Christmas at the cabin in Michigan passed solemnly. Firestone had worked hard to create the wonder of the season, usually their favorite time of the year. Marie had put on a smiley face, but something, someone, was missing.

On New Year's Eve, Firestone brought a new puppy home. *We've been too long without a dog here. Samuel would never stand for it.*

With a steady diet of soup and fresh vegetables, Angel began to regain her physical strength. In the pale light of the Solstice evening, she forced herself to rise and walk to the window. In a white cotton nightgown, she stood framed by moonlight and stared at the endless stars.

Her bare feet grew cold on the plank wood floor. A brief bullet of pain hit her left temple. She lay back down on the quilted bed and felt her growing stomach. She felt life burgeoning inside her. Angel knew she had to protect the baby, keep their child safe and warm, *until Samuel returns.*

New Life

Winter came early and stayed. Isolated by snowfall and a responsibility she had never felt before, Angel spent her days staring through frosty, mullioned windowpanes. Icicles hung from the broad roof edges, and like crystals, changed occasional sunrays into colored patterns on the cedar walls.

Samuel's thirty-three rpm albums rotated constantly on the turntable. His music slowly prodded Angel back to life. She closed her eyes and began to sway to the uplifting voices of the Rascals' "It's a beautiful morning…"

Marie had insisted that Angel use Samuel's attic bedroom retreat. When colored prisms shown on Samuel's desk, Angel imagined him sitting, bent over his writing. When rays of sunlight hit the Martin guitar on its stand, she heard chords being strummed.

The tip of an old fly rod hung suspended in air. The cork handle rested on a book entitled *Trout Madness*. Angel suspected there was more to the book than fishing. Above the book hung a photograph of a ruffed grouse taken by a stream in the Upper Peninsula. Samuel had shot a photo rather than use his shotgun on the proud bird.

Angelique refused to move Samuel's memories. An authentic Navaho bow hung above the closet door. A globe of the world watched over books of every sort. His favorite writers were prominently displayed, where with a glance, he could recall the treasures inside. Heavy, picture frame bookends flanked each end of the shelf above his desk. Firestone, young and strong, guarded the right. Angel studied the prophetic picture of Sally on the left. Samuel's mother, so pretty, yet she held a certain ominous frailty, as if she held back the tide.

The yellow puppy wanted badly to climb the steps to the attic room where other pictures hung strategically placed. Samuel knelt in a fall field with Charlie, a pheasant, and a shotgun. Angelique saw her younger self there, too, in an oval frame above Samuel's desk. She remembered Miss Marianne with a camera the day she left with Ellie for the trip home to St. Simons Island for Christmas. She rubbed her fingers over the smooth, red knife in her pocket.

The dog had learned quickly to "do its business" outside. Each night, Marie lifted the yellow puppy, carried her up the steps, and set her on Samuel's double bed. Angelique lifted one of Sally's quilts before tucking the warm puppy close. She closed her eyes, and breathing slowly like Samuel had taught her, they fell asleep. In the shadow world of dreams, Samuel lay alongside.

When the icy cold of January abated with a thaw, Angel ventured down the stairway into the warmth of the woodstove and her family. She so much wanted to join Firestone on sunny afternoons when he set out on cross country skis. He said he skied for the exercise, but both she and Marie knew better.

Confined by the responsibility of preparing for his son's child, Firestone chafed with boredom. He felt joy in his duty, but also helplessness. His aging testosterone still surged inside and drove a desire he could not quite put his finger on.

He skied alone deep in the woods. He visited Samuel's favorite places. He rested on a boulder that Samuel had shown him. He remembered Samuel telling a tall tale about an old man in the woods who came from nowhere and shared water. Firestone drank sweet homemade wine from a deer hide skin. He waited and searched for a sign.

Down by the creek, two does struggled through the deep snow.

He found a blow hole where a 'pat' might appear. Each time he said 'pat' to himself, he thought, *Partridge, a ruffed grouse, like popple trees are aspen.*

Firestone conjured up an image of Samuel resting on the boulder.

Evenings, they brought out the cribbage board and played three handed. Firestone never let the ladies win. He had never let Samuel win, why should he start now? He did not believe in prizes for participation. How else would the boy have learned? How else would Samuel's aptitude for mathematical probabilities have developed? How else would Samuel have authentically rejoiced when he finally won?

Angel, showing and awkward, began to walk outdoors. During that week-long thaw that comes every winter, she bundled in a barn jacket and pulled on her Mukluk boots. The first day she made the quarter mile hike to the mailbox. She went every day to the mailbox, wishing for news. The yellow puppy tagged along, hopping like a bunny in the snow. Silently, they had agreed, naming dogs was Samuel's job, always had been. Until he returned, Yellow Puppy would suffice.

Marie rejoiced over her daughter's progress, noticing Angel's bright, puffy cheeks and her positive outlook. Firestone noticed, too, but hid in his moments alone, thankful, yet worried. Marie nurtured the strengths of her charges and overlooked any shortcomings. The scent of fresh cinnamon rolls wafted through the house several times a week. Chicken soup simmered regularly, sometimes with noodles, sometimes with rice, often with dumplings. Marie might bake a pot roast with fresh carrots, a casserole with fresh baked tuna, or sharp cheddar and macaroni, and always sweet, yellow onions.

On Sunday mornings, Firestone made his hearty French-Canadian pancakes. He had discovered a recipe for French crepes in another family *Bible*, his grandmother's frayed cookbook, a 1941 edition of Fanny Farmer's *Boston School of Cooking*. Always the experimenter, Firestone substituted whole wheat flower for white and natural brown sugar for processed. He added in cinnamon and a generous pour of Mexican vanilla. Inside the thin, brown crepes, over melted butter, he rolled a fresh sausage link. The final touch, maple syrup from the sugar maples beyond the back field, created a hearty breakfast to carry his family through the day.

Breakfast had always been Samuel's favorite meal, especially on Sundays. But his place at the kitchen table sat empty, and though they all relished the crepes, his presence presided quietly in the room.

On clear winter evenings, when the moon shone over the fields and grapevines, Firestone ventured out on his skis. Orion rose boldly in the south over faraway hills this time of year and eased him into a peaceful state. He thought he was alone, but Marie watched from the front picture window. Angel held the yellow puppy in her arms and looked on through the mullioned panes of her attic room.

Planets arrived and left according to their varying monthly orbits. Firestone paused in the moonlight to identify the orbs. He leaned on his poles and knew somewhere his son watched the same night sky.

Dougal made his entrance when purple Crocus pushed through the last vestige of snow.

Seasonal Shifts

Through Dougal's first summers, the family stayed close to home. Marie always avoided town, never feeling welcomed. In truth, she looked forward to returning to St. Simons. Firestone ran the necessary errands. Occasionally, Angel and the newborn accompanied him, and he beamed with pride when showing off his grandson to his friends in town.

Mostly, they watched the boy grow with the summer sun. When the corn tasseled, Dougal's eyes began to focus. When the first grapes appeared on the vines, Angel plopped on the grass with the boy in her arms and pointed to Papa as he pinched the suckers that stole moisture from the fruit. The boy fought to crawl to the vines, to his grandfather. Marie snuck a glance while hanging bedsheets to dry in the sun or picking the first of the tiny, yellow cherry tomatoes. They all were there when Dougal bit down on a shiny orb and an explosion of goodness set off firecrackers in his mouth. With wondering eyes, Dougal chuckled out loud.

Firestone took care when lifting Dougal in his arms. He never quite forgot the minute shard of shrapnel lodged near his spine. And lately, a raw nerve might send a spark and cause him to wince. Firestone had a healthy respect for soft and vulnerable babies. Marie and Angel held Dougal so gently, yet with controlled strength. Firestone feared his strength, an accidental drop or too tight a hug.

In late August, Firestone picked the short and narrow cobs of sweet corn so tender that blanching hardly seemed necessary. Dougal sat on the grass and chewed on a raw ear while Marie tended the boiling pot so as not to overcook the corn. Angel sliced the hot kernels from the cob into a large mixing bowl with just a touch of butter. Once cooled, they filled freezer bags with blanched corn. A good harvest meant fresh corn through the winter, spring, and into the next early summer, when the garden would again come alive.

In late September, the Pinot grapes sweetened on the vine. Dougal crushed his first handful, put his tiny fist to his mouth, and tasted the nectar. Firestone tended the working must for a week, shooing away the fruit flies that gathered in the warm sunlight. When the week had passed and the must was ready, the family squeezed the last of the juice from the crock and filled two, five-gallon glass carboys with fermenting wine. A week later they racked and fined the wine and set the carboys aside for aging.

Firestone handled the bottling on his own, for as the weather turned cold Up North, hurricane season waned in the south. Marie, Angel, and young Dougal returned to St. Simons Island in October before the first snowfall. Firestone would follow in December, when the wine had been bottled, when he had taken his final trout for the year, and when the leaves had fallen, and ruffed grouse season gave way to the whitetail hunters who stormed his quiet woods in great numbers. He would leave once the pipes had been drained and once he had relished a December snowfall.

Firestone spent Christmas Eve alone by catching up on his reading. He liked to read favorite passages in the *New International Version* in quiet introspection. *A dollop of religion never hurt the soul.* And he missed Samuel, even more so during the Christmas holidays. He worried constantly about his son, and with the others gone, he did not have to hide the worry from his face.

The morning came with a glow over the hills to the south and east. He gazed out the picture window as light caught the tops of the trees on far ridges like cool fire. He followed to the cabin's other windows, each in turn as the living sun moved westward in an elliptical path. In every direction, new trees blazed afire. After a few short minutes, winter clouds dampened the rays, and again he was alone. He wished he had gone south with the ladies and his grandson. *Why do I always withdraw from people?*

No matter, the world will be here tomorrow when I wake.

Firestone had pursued the quest to find his son. The detective he had hired had tracked Samuel as far as Bear Butte, given the clues Angel had provided. The trail ended, stymied by the Black Hills.

Firestone had made the trek to the Dakotas himself in August to no outcome other than the memories of meeting Sally so many years ago. He wished he had not told the children about Bear Butte. *Might Samuel have come home?*

Firestone harbored no blame for Angel. So young and scared, she would never intentionally hurt anyone. He knew in his heart that Samuel sought his essence in the West, just as Firestone had. The power of the Good Mountain had called upon his son after Angel had left him.

The Great Spirit would help and guide him through his troubles.

A January-like thaw came early, two days after Christmas. Temperatures in the forties allowed an all-night rain to melt the snow. Firestone woke to a green morning reminiscent of March. Another day and the rain would freeze to ice. He was needed down south. The boy needed a man's presence, and who better to fill in for his father than his grandfather? The family would return north in May and plant the vegetable garden on Dougal's birthday.

And so it was that the bounty of brief Michigan summers and glorious autumns gave way to the salt air and seawater of Saint Simon's ocean beaches as seasons shifted with the sun.

Chapter Twelve:
Canada
1973-1974

SAFE PASSAGE

Libby returned from town with pasta and a few other staples. Samuel entered the kitchen from chores to the pleasant smell of her tuna fish casserole baking in the oven. He enjoyed her version even though she used canned fish instead of fish fresh from the ocean as Marie had. She had feed supplement for the sheep and a jar of Bag Balm to treat Maggie's growing teats. A breeder from Missoula had brought his stud up to the ranch the previous month, and inside Maggie grew her second purebred litter. The pups would provide some extra needed cash.

Libby had also stopped by a stationary store to pick up a leather-bound journal and a few good pens. Samuel met the truck in the yard, followed by a waddling dog.

"For you," she handed the journal to Samuel. "Write down those thoughts that circle through your mind. You sure don't repeat them out loud."

Samuel took to writing like the proverbial duck takes to water. He scribbled thoughts in the mornings before chores and again in the exaggerated dusk of evening. Midday, when they stopped for lunch, he would excuse himself from the table to jot down a few thoughts or key words, so that later he could remember and picture a scene in his head.

Seven pups arrived in August, just after the second cutting of hay grasses. Samuel held Maggie as she struggled with each push, then let her lick and clean the newborns. Libby moved them, each in turn, to make room for the next, and to keep Maggie from accidentally hurting them in her movement.

Interested buyers began calling and coming by the ranch. The breeder made the trip from Missoula to study his pick of the males. That was their deal; he raised the stud, thus got the pick of the males, but Libby controlled the female pups. She would only let a fertile female go to another breeder, and the price was steep.

The Sheriff stopped by more often, too. His structured way worried Samuel. He thought like a cop, all black and white, no variance. A thing was either right or wrong; lawful or unlawful. He enforced the law.

"So, what are your plans for the fall, young Mr. Firestone?"

Samuel had never given out his real last name, Thompson.

The sheriff clearly wanted him out of the way. Samuel took too much of Lisbeth's attention. Watson had not yet put out feelers on Samuel, but the thought had occurred to him.

"You let the boy be," Libby interjected, knowing that Samuel hid something beneath the surface. "He can stay as long as he wants."

Yet in her heart, Libby knew that Samuel couldn't stay for long. The Sheriff would surely keep digging and expose the deep secret that Samuel kept to himself. And she was becoming too attached. He might get hurt, and she could not abide the loss of another boy.

In the fall, coincidentally near the time that Angelique and Dougal were heading south to St. Simon's Island, a woman arrived at the ranch. She drove a Ford van that had been converted for road living. Libby had often spoken to Samuel of her friend, Alexandra, who also bred Scottish Wolfhounds. Alex hailed from Graham, Ontario, and had made the long drive alone to pick up a female pup. Alex and Libby were the best of old friends, the kind who don't fret over what to say, or not say. Their bond had only increased with Linc's passing. They spoke on the phone every week, and a visit was something both cherished. Libby had a favor to ask.

"Alex will be staying a few days, but tonight we'll celebrate. Samuel, please get the grill burning. Fresh lamb chops need a hot, fast fire."

Libby uncorked a bottle of deep purple California cabernet that she had been saving for a special occasion. She poured a glass for Alex and one for herself. They sat on the porch admiring the young man carefully stacking charcoal on the Weber.

"Dearest friend, I'd like you to take Samuel home with you to Canada."

Libby nearly lost her balance after a longing embrace. She wiped a tear from Samuel's cheek with her coarse fingers.

"Come back. Come back and see me someday, when you can."

"I have a feeling we'll see each other again."

Alex and Samuel crossed the international border at the nearest point, on Highway 24, just south of Kildeer, Saskatchewan. The border guard knew Libby well and briefly scanned the puppy's papers before letting the van pass through.

North Ontario

Samuel had become accustomed to heavy snow. In the good winter days at the cabin near Petoskey, the lake effect often dumped twenty inches or more unexpectedly. Forecasters tried to predict the amount of snowfall, but they only guessed. In December and January, before Lake Michigan froze, cold air from the arctic blew across warm open water and drew the moisture up into the clouds. Once the winds hit the sandy dune shoreline, the clouds dropped their water-laden burden upon the land. Sometimes the snow did not fall, but the weatherman always hedged his prediction with a range: a trace to three inches, two to four, three to ten, perhaps a foot.

Canadian snow was different. Storms came from the arctic but not across a great lake. Alex and Samuel heard no faulty predictions. They never watched the television weatherman. Only sketchy television signals reached northern Ontario. A wet, heavy snow fell almost every night, dropping a few more inches. By the middle of January, the banks along the driveway had reached twelve feet on both sides, leaving nowhere to push the new snow except onto the gravel Provincial Road. Alex unnecessarily worried that the plow driver would block the entrance by the mailbox.

But Alex knew the plow driver. She knew every one of the nearly one hundred-twenty souls that lived year-round within a forty-mile radius of the general store. Most catered to the tourist trade. The small inland lakes that dotted the map held an abundance of fish, mostly walleye. A fisherman had to go all the way down to Nipigon to catch the huge, lake-run brook trout that swam the river to Lake Superior. On each of these smaller lakes, a few part-time guides maintained rustic resort cabins with their families. The influx arrived each summer and stayed from the melting in June until the snows returned in autumn.

And with early fall came the hunters. Ducks by the thousands, perhaps millions, migrated from subarctic potholes down the flyways of Manitoba. Most stopped to feed and rest on Lake Winnpigosis. The flocks bifurcated, some east to Lake Superior, then down the Great Lakes to southern Ontario and Ohio. Other flocks split more southerly, with an aerial view of Lake of the Woods, Minnesota, before continuing down the Mississippi River to Arkansas and the southern Gulf bayous.

Some hunters came for the moose, mostly from the States, where the moose populations had been run out by civilization. The Royal Canadian Mounties kept a close eye on these visitors to control trafficking of guns, moose mounts, and meat. One moose kill to a customer, and the hunter better be registered.

Winter came and stayed long that far north. Samuel and Alex grew close by necessity. A tall, thin woman, she cropped her hair short like a man's, reminding Samuel of an older Joan Baez. Alex, who had a special sense for reading others' thoughts, tried to keep Samuel occupied with chores and physical labor to take his mind from his brooding secret. The dogs and horses required constant care. And cords of firewood burned quickly.

Alex kept an eccentric library, and Samuel read whenever he had a chance. He tried to make sense of Castenada's *Teachings of Don Juan* trilogy and came away with a new appreciation for crows. Samuel would never look at a crow the same again. Alex's taste also encompassed environmental awareness. Samuel read all she had of Edward Abbey and worked his way through Rachel Carson's *Silent Spring.*

Books took his mind away from home and helped him sleep. He had become almost paranoid with worry, afraid to make contact, afraid of what his father might think of his running away. He tried to put Angelique out of his mind, but she always returned in some form. A character in a book or a scene on the ocean or in the woods often caused his mind to wander.

In the spring, Alex introduced Samuel to her nephew who lived a few hours west. Clarence ran a duck hunting and fishing lodge over in Manitoba. His wife Della cleaned, cooked, and packed lunches for the guests. Her sister Daphne helped out, too. Clarence had inherited the lodge from his father when Alex's brother Joseph drowned.

Joseph and Clarence had gone out on the river to ice fish two winters past. The ice cracked. Joseph slipped in and was carried under by the current. Clarence ran downstream over the glass clear ice and followed his father's shape clawing and scratching at the glass ceiling, until the clawing stopped. Joseph's body came up in the spring, down by Meadow Portage.

Alex had a premonition that Clarence and Samuel would be good company for one another. Clarence would have a man friend who shared loss. Someone to confide in. And Samuel, a good listener, would have a new challenge to keep his mind busy. In August, Samuel traveled to Manitoba to work for Clarence.

Samuel fit in with the young survivors. Though he constantly thought about Angelique, Marie, and his father, all back in Michigan or down at St. Simons, he found new friends. He learned to guide for the duck hunters. His skill with animals helped, as the lodge's big black Labrador Retriever claimed Samuel as his own. Bucky swam like no other dog Samuel had ever seen, through the unpredictable currents that weaved between small grass islands in the broad delta below the lodge. Ten knots of current ran in spots, and Bucky still made progress upstream with a prize canvasback carried gently in his jaws.

In the evenings, Samuel sat in with one of Clarence's guitars while Daphne entertained the guests with a smooth and heartfelt version of "Strawberry Wine." A beautiful, long-legged, golden-haired seventeen years, she had the hunters and fishermen eating out of her hands.

One night after the guests had retired, after a shared joint and Clarence and Della had retreated to their bedroom, Daphne eased into Samuels' arms. They caressed on the leather sofa, and Daphne nibbled at Samuel's ear. He held her tightly and enjoyed the warmth, yet he resisted. Even in that moment, he saw only Angelique.

Della shook the fully clothed pair awake early the next morning, "Up and at em'; you two, the guests are here for breakfast."

In early November, when the guests stopped coming, Alex drove the van over from Ontario. Her arthritis had kicked in, and she needed help back at her place on the lake to make it through the winter. Samuel had so enjoyed the company of young folks to take his mind off his troubles, but his responsible nature prevailed.

As they were leaving, Bucky tried to climb in the van. Samuel stopped several times along the driveway to shoo him back. At the Province road, Bucky finally stopped and sat on his broad haunches, watching the van fade into the prairie.

Back on the frozen lake, Samuel, who always looked on the bright side, found himself dealing with a new emotion. He fought to put his finger on these feelings. The long winter seemed to grow longer, to crawl like the snowdrifts that piled so high that they might never melt. Spring might never come. He longed for St. Simons Island. He wanted the salt water to wash over his feet while he fished on the beach. He wanted Angelique to bring a sandwich and sit with him in the sand. Samuel needed the feel of a warm ocean breeze to fill the sails of *Wanderer* and carry him to an anchorage in a protected bay off Cumberland Island, where wild ponies and porpoise calmed the earth.

THE VISION

Samuel dreamed and slept through until dawn. He had gone to bed tired the night before, and as Alex had suggested, placed two fingers on his forehead in order to calm his higher self. But in a misty dawn, he was unable to remember the dreams. Confusion reigned. Only by lying still on his back and closing his eyes could he regain his equilibrium.

The sweet spring-song of cardinals carried through the morning fog. Blue jays answered from the nearby red pine wood. Samuel climbed up to face the day. After strong coffee and a shave, he sat on the porch and again contemplated his dream.

People noises bothered him. Clanging pots, dishes being washed, and the muted voices of too-polite conversation in another room echoed in his head and disturbed the soothing birdsong. A red-bellied woodpecker swooped down to the feeder outside his window, and in a break from the clanging, Samuel heard grey, black, and white wings moving air. Still the birds sang in the woods and awaited a sun that was sure to break through the morning mist.

Deep in his soul, Samuel knew something lived out there. He had a hard time explaining his beliefs, but when chickadees chirped, or a red-tailed hawk perched in the popple tree that grew on a thirty-degree angle and hung over an abandoned pasture, he felt a message. Other times, a bald eagle took over the perch and the hawks stayed away.

The yearling pup Samuel had named Libby's Stella, had come to his bedside and her panting awakened him. He put on his moccasins and followed the dog out on the front porch. Stella rushed to gobble early white clover petals that grew in the shade beneath a flowering lilac bush. Samuel looked up at the southern sky, where Jupiter shone juxtaposed with Saturn like the eyes of a grand wolf looking down upon the earth. He left Stella out to solve her unrest and returned to his bed. Unable to sleep, he read until dawn brightened the yard and a lone bird whistled through his window from the woods. He could not identify the birdsong, but somehow eased, turned off the bed lamp.

Alexandra interpreted dreams. She read Samuel his horoscope religiously, though he was never quite convinced. He mostly didn't believe, but sometimes the words echoed truth. He took signs where offered, and his sixth sense, one that combined all the other five, rarely led him astray. Yet often, he out-thought the message. His desire could over-power thought and he knew trouble generally followed rationalization.

Samuel reached into the bin of sunflower seeds and filled a pitcher full. He restocked the iron bird feeder that hung on a chain outside the window of his small corner room. He opened the feeder's top and studied the ornamental iron, faux finch that perched, tack-welded, life-like. *Did visiting birds think the iron finch was alive?*

As he began to pour the seeds, a hummingbird buzzed in close to his face, hovered, and looked directly into his hazel green eyes. *A young hummer*, he thought, small, and still growing, with bright red feathers surrounded by black and white. He felt reassured by the buzzing of the bird's tiny wings. The little bird shared an intimate moment, brief and powerful, and lifted Samuel's spirits before flying away in retreat, the bird's presence only a memory.

Samuel could be that way. He could smile and his glow could brighten someone's day. The next moment, he might appear aloof and distant, his mind lost in thought. If asked a question, he stared blankly at the sky and often took too long to answer, a trait others found confounding. Frustrated by Samuel's apparent insensibility, they would move on to their next thought while Samuel still considered the first question and agonized over an answer.

A pair of Sandhill cranes flew high overhead like two prurient, Olympic divers who never hit the water. He thought of a story in last week's Sunday newspaper. Two young girls died in a car crash on an icy bridge. Beautiful beings who live in the spirit world and become messengers and fill the void between then and now. The cranes re-minded Samuel that life may change forms, but nothing ever dies.

On clear, chilled nights, Samuel and Alex walked down to the lake and quietly studied the stars. Billions and more pins of light sent meaning, the warmth of eternity. Samuel could never interpret an exact message, yet he knew when to feel safe and when to be concerned.

Alexandra felt the worry deep in Samuel's soul. She also read his strength of character. She knew that he hid the truth, but for a reason, a good reason.

Visions confirmed her suspicions, but she kept them to herself, waiting for him to ask. Samuel had become part of her family. Alex watched the way he stared at the birds, the way a chickadee might land in his hand, and the way he communicated with his eyes. Dogs rallied around him. Samuel had become so helpful in raising the Wolfhound pups. He gentled them by seven weeks. Libby's Stella, the bitch that came with Samuel from the States, allowed him in with the newborns, and even seemed to understand when one was taken away.

In addition to room and board, Alex paid Samuel what she could. He saved his pay and the tips he'd made in Manitoba. He had his eye on a well-used Dodge, a step side truck with a *For Sale* sign in the window. The forest green pickup sat next to the general store in the village. Alex told him that a young American returning home to the lower States from Alaska had left the truck with the store owner in trade for a newer Chevy. The merchant had made out well with a good sum of cash from the young man who had been up at the oil fields in Prudhoe Bay. Painted a dark, pearly green with a matching topper, the truck ran on a solid, slant-six powertrain. Twelve hundred Canadian could take her. Alex let Samuel work off the final two hundred.

Alexandra often saw auras hover about a person. Samuel's aura, of course, glowed with an almost sparkling mist. Other, darker auras portended danger. Samuel often helped confirm her conclusions. Occasionally, a young man might come along to buy a pup, clearly for the wrong reasons. She knew by the way he walked toward them. Her eyes met Samuel's, and together they knew.

"Sorry," she would say, "this litter is promised."

One warm afternoon, a blue pickup truck with Wisconsin plates rumbled up the drive. A particularly sketchy character got out and kicked the door shut. His partner, also with long stringy hair and sporting three days of whisker growth, jumped out the passenger door and lowered the tailgate. Corrugated metal cages had been installed in the pickup bed. A pair of Plott Hounds howled from one of the cages.

Fortunately, Samuel had delayed his trip to Manitoba to work with Clarence at the duck-hunting lodge. In the States, they were celebrating Labor Day Weekend, and this questionable pair hunted bears with dogs. Rather, the dogs chased a bear until cornered. The men then tracked their dogs with radio collars until they got close enough to hear the incessant barking. Invariably, when they caught up to the noise, the hounds howled beneath a tree where a scared and helpless black bear hung in the branches. One lucky hunter then calmly aimed and shot, careful not to tear up the hide.

"I'd like to buy two of those Wolfhounds from ya', one stud, and one bitch. The wolves have been killing my Plott Hounds. I need tougher dogs."

Alex removed her leather gloves. She and Samuel had been picking the sweetcorn from her garden to put up for the winter. She wondered how this pair had ever been allowed to cross the border into Ontario. She spotted two rifles hanging on a rack in the pickup window.

"Sorry, the pups are all spoken for."

"Money talks, and bullshit walks," the man replied. "I'll give you five-hundred American each."

"Sorry, but like I said, the dogs have been promised."

The other man walked toward Alex, who had moved toward the shed that housed the kennel. Several pups played in the grass behind the gate. Choke collars dangled from each of his large, dirty hands.

"Look lady, we'll pay you, but we're taking two dogs."

Samuel stepped down from the front porch. In his arms, he held the double-barreled Fox side-by-side that always hung on a rack by the front door. He fired one barrel high out over the lake and reloaded.

"Hold on now, buddy, we're outta' here," the first man yelled, as the other fumbled with the door handle on the passenger side.

Alex hurried to the house and called the local constable who relayed her description to the Mounted Police. Samuel kept the Fox handy while they returned to the work in the garden.

The constable called back that evening, "Caught up with those two on the way to Thunder Bay. Their guns are forfeit. They'll cool off in a cell tonight and be escorted back to the border in the morning. Won't bother you anymore, eh?"

Sleep came uneasily to Alexandra. While in and out of fitful tossing and turning, she received a premonition. She saw Samuel with a dark-skinned girl somewhere on a beach. Wild ponies watched from a distance. Porpoise rose from the sea and showed their eyes. A young boy chased a tiny girl through white sand while she played in shallow, greenish-blue surf.

After the vision, she slept soundly. When Alex woke in the morning, Samuel's truck was gone. Duck season had begun over at Clarence's lodge in Manitoba.

Another season passed before she told him what she had seen. The day a letter arrived from Libby in Montana, she had the vision again.

THE LETTER

Samuel took a moment's rest on a cedar chair on the porch. He had been working in Alex's yard all morning, and as the June sun warmed, he enjoyed a glass of water fresh from the well. The latest litter of pups had been placed, and Libby's Stella lay down with her chin on his boots.

Honeybees buzzed at pink buds that sprouted from the bushes surrounding the porch. If he held perfectly still, an occasional hummingbird might come to the sweet sugar water in the glass tube that hung on a chain. Sometimes a bee ventured too deep into the glass while chasing the false nectar. If Samuel was quick enough to react, he might free the trapped fuzzy form before it drowned in sugar water.

He wondered why he was never stung. The bees' humming grew ever stronger and created a natural vibration in his universe. Perhaps because he showed no fear? If a bee landed on him, he would gently brush it away toward the sky. Stella, on the other hand, would snap at the bee if it came too close. She occasionally caught one in her mouth and chewed. Nearly as often she whined when the bee won the battle and stung her muzzle.

Alexandra pushed open the wooden screen door at the sound of tires on the gravel drive. The post carrier began to walk to the porch where the mailbox hung on the wall, but he stopped several yards away upon hearing loud buzzing.

"Here's your post, eh? I'll not be coming any closer."

Stella let out a low growl when Samuel rousted her to walk down the steps. He thanked the postman, waved, and handed several letters to Alex, who had settled in the other chair on the porch.

"Probably more bills," Alex complained. "Oh, wait, here's one from Libby."

She tore the envelope open and scanned through the elegant cursive.

"All is well," she says. "A new litter. She wants me to bring Stella down during her next cycle. Tell Samuel, she writes, the U.S. is pulling out of Vietnam. The draft will be ending."

Chapter Thirteen:
Generations
1974

The Child

Marie chased the giggling child from the living room. The wooden screen door slammed against the frame behind her. The movement of the door broke the still warmth of late spring in the islands.

A dog gate across the steps allowed Dougal to safely play on the cottage's broad porch. The child tended to wander. Sometimes Marie tied a light rope around his waist while he explored the yard. Other times he sat on the sandy grass and studied budding wildflowers. Bees circled harmlessly about, never landing on him.

He had learned to talk and walk simultaneously at nine months. At just past two years, Dougal's vocabulary nearly surpassed Marie's, in English. She also taught him her island variety French. His curiosity knew no bounds.

He climbed on his grandfather's lap, and if Firestone dared to look away, Dougal took Papa's chin in both of his small hands. He demanded direct, unfettered eye contact.

"A bright lad, like your father," Firestone would say.

"Aye, Papa," the boy replied.

Another spring approached, and in his habitual migration, Firestone traveled north ahead of the family to prepare the cabin for the summer.

Maybe this spring, maybe Samuel will come home.

The River

Firestone leaned back on the open tailgate of his old step side Ford pickup. He pulled off his left boot and struggled to fit one leg into his waders. He always began the day, or any adventure, with his left foot. But now he had one leg buried in the waders and the other sticking out with his right shoe still firmly affixed below.

Firestone had become a creature of habits who had forgotten the order of his habits. He had prepared to fish countless times in his life, but continued to learn the hard way to take his time in the preparation.

Time might be saved in the end.

Without letting the waders touch the ground, he reached down to work the wading boot over wetsuit-like toes and felt a new muscle twinge in his upper back, followed by a shooting pain in his shoulder.

Just a passing shot.

He stood straight up and took a deep breath. A different muscle, this time somewhere in his lower back, twitched and strained when he grabbed the suspender clasp too quickly. He liked these new waders, the kind with a separate boot. The boot gave him support wading over uneven river bottoms, over rocks rounded from a thousand years of current. He thought of his first set of heavy rubber waders with attached boots that leaked and never fit quite right. His feet constantly ached, but the thrill of catching a trout always took the pain from his mind.

He assembled his four-part fly rod and tied on a brown drake imitation while noticing that he'd need a new leader soon. The tiny, three-circle knot broke off in his teeth twice before he tried a fourth loop and finally felt the tightness of a turn that would hold a trout.

He took a few extra flies in a small box and made sure the box was zipped into the pocket of his vest along with a squeeze bottle of bug dope and some fly-drying dust. In another vest pocket, he carried two smokes protected in an old cigar tube along with a cheap lighter. He also kept several partially used packs of wooden matches in various pockets.

You never know.

As he followed a lightly worn deer path down a short ridge toward the river, he guided the fragile tip of his seven-foot rod through the perils of bushes that seemed to want to snatch the hook on the fly and bend the rod tip. At the bottom of the draw, tag alders had been split apart by deer crossing the stream. He walked boldly, and with just a moment's study, decided to step backward into the water while supporting his weight by grabbing alder branches that appeared to be growing solidly into the bank. Alternatively, he might sit on the bank's black mud and slowly rise to his feet while balancing in the current. Firestone never liked to get mud on his waders if he could help it. The alder branches held fast.

A cedar waxwing fluttered in the alder leaves as he let go. His foot slipped on a submerged branch that caught his toe. He paused, took a breath, and regained his balance. The water flowed above his knees but well below his waist, and the gravelly bottom that encourages spawning trout made for a firm base.

Firestone paused to watch the silvery-grey bird fly down the river.

He stood out in the middle of the current for a long while to center his balance and his thoughts. His life had become bothersome lately, a roller coaster of boredom and worry followed by brief moments of ecstasy. He had been sleeping later, probably a result of re-reading favorite texts too late into the night. Some stories never grew old, while most new writers who caused a sensation in the publishing world bored him. Whiny, young writers wrote of the death of a parent, as if no one ever dies.

Get over it.

Firestone considered brilliance as rare as a twenty-inch brook trout taken from a small stream, like the one where he stood. Experience creates a story, not study, nor a command of grammar. Modern writers crawled like lemmings to imitate the latest craze and fell into the abyss of banality. *And critics,* he thought, *who made them God?*

He took another deep breath to let bad thoughts ease away into the endless forest on the far bank of the river.

He heard a gulp and turned his head downstream toward a bend where water swirled with the contour before backing up in an eddy. An expanding circle emanated from a spot in the center of the dark water where a trout had risen.

Firestone surveyed the bank and tried to read the river depth to find a route to the bend. He decided that the other side would work best. He trudged through the water, making far too much noise. In his younger days, he had crept silently upon a likely hole. He had been lighter on his feet then; heavy still, and muscular, but agile and in control. He had seen death in his youth and became numb to the dying. Women had lived and gone before him; Samuel's mother, the first, who left in the glory of bearing a son. She was a lovely creature, but too fragile for this world. Firestone smiled on the happy times and could hardly fault the later times after she had gone, when he dedicated his life to raising Samuel. Only the deep recesses of a lonely night or standing still in the river might offer time to miss Sally.

He longed to see his boy, but somehow knew Samuel was safe. Samuel had grown without a mother, and now young Dougal, approaching his fourth year, needed his father.

Firestone waded carefully close to the far bank. Sand and muck had built up above the bend. He found himself balancing on a steep edge that dropped off into dark water that was certainly over his head and would fill his waders should he slip. His feet began to sink in the muck, so he moved faster to avoid the suction. He knew that he would have to return this same way, to repeat his steps, and thought how stupid he could be for an old man, risking all for the chance at a tiny, iridescent fish.

With waning energy, he lurched onto the steep, soft bank, dug the fingers of his left hand into the muck, and pulled himself up the final few feet. His footing gave way with the effort, and he landed face down in black mud. In his right hand, he held his fly rod high, the way a mother might protect her baby.

He tossed the rod up into long grass and attempted a two-handed push-up to clear the ground. As he gained momentum, he looked down, and adjacent to the indentation left by his own hands, he noticed deep claw marks etched into the mud. Another creature had attempted this same crossing, and Firestone knew, in these familiar environs, only a black bear left such tracks.

Finding a firm edge, he sat on the bank, dangled the legs of his waders into the clear water, and reached into his top vest pocket for a lighter and a smoke. The river cleaned the black earthy silt from his legs but dissolved into a dirty swirl that floated into the bend and eddied into the hole where he had seen the fish rise. Like the cloud of murky water he watched dissipate, the women who had followed Samuel's mother faded away. Though Marie had filled his life in recent years, in his private thoughts, he had always returned to Sally, in the time before Samuel.

Before Marie, thoughts had often got the better of him, and so very alone, drink became his companion. Whiskey-soaked frustration turned to rage, and he struck out at whatever or whomever stood close. In the fresh light of morning, he had felt an apology present, but unspoken. He had no time to worry about anyone other than Samuel. He retreated to nature, his grapevines, his daily chores, and if lucky, to the river.

Marie understood the origin of Firestone's shortcomings.

I am thankful that she set my faults aside.

The river flattened out and returned to gravel downstream. Firestone blew smoke rings, waiting to let the hole and his muddied mind settle.

Waiting, an admirable trait, he thought, one he had practiced early in life but had to relearn from Samuel. A child learns, then teaches. Samuel seemed to have an innate understanding of patience, while Firestone had no time to enjoy such luxury. He had worked his whole life; his life was his work. That, and raising his son alone. He took pleasure, though, in the knowledge that his son understood the sacrifices he had made.

And he and Samuel had always been friends.

He had spoiled Samuel by trying to fill both roles, a fatherly mother and a motherly father. But Samuel had grown up early. He was always the smartest in school, though he easily grew bored with teachers and developed a firm disposition against the abuse of authority. Samuel had struck out on his own even as a young boy. He had hitchhiked cross country several times before his fifteenth birthday and traveled through Europe on his own at nineteen.

Firestone asked, "Where are you bumming to this time," and the tone in his voice was slanted purposefully, with the emphasis on "bum." *But Samuel had always returned home.*

Firestone knew that Samuel laughed but listened to the lessons hidden in his admonitions, like one of his favorite quips, "What are ya gonna' do, shovel shit?"

Firestone's folksy wisdom had been born of his own experiences in life, in coming of age during the depression, and in creating a comfortable life. He taught Samuel and Samuel would teach Dougal.

High above the river, a white arrow broke the blue May sky, a contrail from a lone jet following a great circle route to the west coast. He thought of the days running trucks across the border to Canada, running molasses for booze, a country boy fresh from the north woods, running from the feds. Firestone still favored Canadian whiskey.

After the war and after she died, he took Samuel south to grow up in the Georgia barrier islands, where he had promised to take Sally, though he never did. But always present in spirit, she watched over their son.

When Samuel was old enough, Firestone had closed up the cabin, set aside mementos, and hid reminders. He fastened boards over the windows and doors. He and his young son had driven an out-of-the-way route through Canada, thence south along the East Coast, to reach a new life in a different place, a cottage near the sea. He tried to raise Samuel as he knew Sally would have wanted.

Firestone watched the lovely cedar wax wing trade up and down the river with tufted head, the demure merging of natural, silvery grey feathers. A messenger for the aware fisherman, the bird foretold a hatch. He had worked his way downriver into a broad bend. He stood on a rocky run, his boots barely covered by clear water. He gauged the air and tried to grasp one of the hatching bugs that floated nervously above the surface, wondering if the bug knew his brief time on earth had ended.

His polarized lenses changed the color of things.

Seeing through rose-colored glasses.

He chuckled, always feeling better after laughing at himself. Firestone recognized his smallness in the world. A bit of humility never hurts. He took the glasses off and discovered mahogany flies hatching. Almost purple, like the purple finch he had seen the other day at his feeder, a natural, brilliant purple, yet never gaudy. In his fly box, he had a similar fly.

The river flowed down through a bend perhaps forty feet away. Good tree clearance would make for an easy cast. Near the far shore, he could tell the dark water deepened with the run. A dead spruce hung and bobbed over the downstream bank. Behind him, a cedar tree had fallen into the river and created a small island that caused the flow to bifurcate above, before re-joining below, where he stood.

If you see a path, take it, as Yogi Berra said.

The river takes the path that it must, one of least resistance, the only path available. The path might change tomorrow. A little rain, or not enough rain, and the river would become a different place.

Perhaps people change in the same way?

But like the river with a gravity bottom, a base beneath which the river does not flow, Firestone thought that a person's basic nature remains constant. Though he had fished this river and others, many times in youth, in middle age, and now in greying years, the river was always new, and he was always young and overwhelmed by the power of moving water.

He sent a flawless cast. The mahogany fly floated in the current naturally, so much like a dying insect who has spent his short life looking for a mate, a partner.

To procreate is to live.

Samuel had made Firestone's life hard at times, yet never too hard, such that he overlooked the grand and mysterious gift he had been given. Now Samuel had fathered a child, Firestone's grandson, who smiled so happily, so like his mother, Angelique.

In his own silent way, Firestone prayed that the fate which had befallen him, losing his wife at such a young age, would never reoccur in his line. Samuel had missed the idea of a mother. He would never understand the warmth that only a mother's hug can provide.

Firestone believed Samuel would return soon. If Samuel had known that he had fathered a son, nothing could stop him.

The mahogany floated in a moving patch of still water until the dry fly reached a log jutting out from the bank. There, the current funneled into small rippling waves that followed the log diagonally toward the center of the stream. The fly dragged under the surface, became waterlogged, and disappeared. Firestone raised his rod and drew the fly from the river. He false cast several times over his head to dry out the imitation insect before laying it out once again at the head of the current. He watched while the faux-insect drifted downstream.

He repeated the process several times even though he saw no indication of fish rising, until becoming distracted while drawing back on the rod, he turned ever so slightly toward the bank. Firestone stumbled and lost his rhythm. He tugged on the rod and felt too much weight on the tip. A closer inspection indicated a shit-tangle of knots. He sat on a grassy bank to undo the nylon bird's nest.

Nothing like messing up a cast to bring a man back to earth.

Slow down, once again, slow down. A momentary lapse in concentration and look what happens. A lesson he would like to teach his son. But Samuel would have to learn, in his own way, in his own good time. Firestone conjured up Samuel's face, a smiling face, and buried somewhere deep in Samuel's features, he saw her. Sally hadn't really left. He saw her nose and her wise yet distant countenance. He knew that Sally had loved him. She had revealed her innermost dreams while never truly giving up her independence.

Firestone began his way back upstream with the fly taut at the end of his rod to avoid overhanging alders. He ducked under an ash branch, a widow-maker, and scrambled quickly up the bank using the sides of a beaver run for leverage. The bear had crossed there, a fact made evident by several toe marks in the mud. Firestone hadn't smelled anything foul, so he proceeded unworried across a peninsula of low growth that had been created by the bend of the river. He proceeded with a mission, back toward the pool where he had first seen a trout rise.

Quietly, he sat on a log and studied the dark water. The trout rose once again with a slurp. A repeating, concentric circular pattern moved outwardly, and slowly the surface settled back into stillness. He waited. The trout rose. The pattern resettled. He stood, quietly prepped his rod, and cast to the pool's far bank.

A torpedo like shape hit the mahogany fly on his way up and without pause continued the trajectory. His complete length shimmered above the water's surface as the trout, a twenty-four-inch brown, struggled like an overloaded airplane to gain lift before reversing course down, deep down, into the river's rust-iron depths.

Firestone let the fish run out until he felt an ever-so-slight pause in the pull, and then he clasped the bright green fly line against the rod with his thumb while simultaneously walking down the bank and into the river. He ignored claw marks marking the muddy bank where he entered. He thought of the wild fish fighting for life at the end of his line. He thought of his wife dying so very young, and his son, Samuel, fighting to live life with the same vigor as the fish.

He slowly pulled the trout toward the bank where his waders sank into the muck. A large maple sweeper branch broke off upstream, drifted into the pool, and caught his leg beneath the surface, yet still he reeled in, determined to see the colorful trout up close. Firestone exhaled, satisfied. He held the trout in his left hand and freed the hook with his right while his waders filled with water, and the sandy muck of the earth pulled at his feet, drawing him ever downward.

Finally realizing his predicament, Firestone struggled against the current while releasing the beautiful, brown trout. Watching the fish slip away, he took a deep breath and submerged, attempting to free the heel of his wader from the solid branch drawing him down.

Clouded as in a dream, Marie and Hector waved from the porch at St. Simons.

Hands clasped, Samuel and Angelique watched over Dougal while his grandson picked the first grapes of autumn.

As Firestone's head went under, a red cardinal perched on overhanging maple branches above the distortion of iron-tinged water. Sally's face shone brightly through the mist before fading into a collage. The Good Mountain formed a backdrop as Sally smiled, like the first time he saw her.

How can this be, he wondered, as he followed, floating free of this world.

Chapter Fourteen:
Ashes and Grapevines
1974

Notice

After sending the good news of the war's end north, Libby had tracked Samuel's real identity down at the town library. She kept her findings to herself and sent off for the newspaper from Petoskey, Michigan.

She had to use all her accumulated good will with the border guards to arrange Samuel's passage across in a Dodge pickup that was registered in Ontario. Alexandra followed in her van while Libby's Stella rode with Samuel in the truck. Libby waited at the international border, having delivered two fresh-baked apple pies, one for each of the agents on duty.

"This is just between us," she told them, "No need for the Sheriff to know."

Back at the ranch, Libby prepared a turkey dinner, including Samuel's favorite cranberry stuffing and thick, rich gravy. The three of them shared a half gallon bottle of Gallo red table wine and laughed into the night.

"Better than my father's wine." Samuel's thoughts slipped out. "Though Firestone's brew works better as a cordial to be sipped after dinner. Some years ferment better than others."

Both happy to have been entrusted with at least some of Samuel's truth, the ladies gently joined hands and retired to Libby's bedroom. Samuel cuddled up in his old room, with Maggie and Libby's Stella resting on the rag rug at the foot of his bed.

With the next day's mail, a Petoskey newspaper arrived. Libby scanned the news quickly before her eyes locked on the Death Notices.

"Firestone Thompson, age 62, passed away on May 7th at his cabin in the Upper Peninsula. He is survived by his son, Samuel Firestone Thompson, and grandson, Dougal Dee Thompson. Complete Obituary to follow."

Escanaba River

Alone with his thoughts on his way home from Libby's ranch, Samuel took a country route, US Highway 2, across northern Montana and North Dakota. He stopped often to stretch, and when he reached Minnesota, stayed awhile along the Red River of the North. He drove without sleeping until he found a familiar park in Wisconsin along the St. Croix River.

A Michigan State Trooper had taken Firestone's remains to a funeral home in Iron Mountain. The body had been cremated. Samuel thanked the odd-looking undertaker and carefully set the quart-sized clay pot on the passenger seat of his Dodge pickup.

Papa will enjoy our ride, like the first trip we took together, south to St. Simons Island.

Sunlight reflected from the mirror on the step side Dodge parked in the grass by the cabin on the Escanaba River. Samuel fired up the woodstove against the coming cold of a late spring night in the Upper Peninsula. Papa had already mounted the handle on the point-well pump. Samuel recalled his father's words:
You have to break the pump down each fall so the works won't freeze.

He took a half full bottle of the Glenlivet from the cupboard below the sink and poured three fingers into a glass. He walked to the porch, lit one of his father's smokes, eased himself into a chair, and considered the clay urn.
A pair of red squirrels chattered in the spruce above the birdfeeder. A bold Canadian Jay swooped in for a landing. A doe and spotted fawn licked at the salt block that Firestone had tossed into the clearing across the river.

Samuel rolled the scotch around in his numbed mouth to take the edge off before swallowing. He reached into the urn and lifted a handful of course, grey dust. He walked to the riverbank, said a silent prayer, and tossed a piece of his father into the wind. Ashes slowly dissolved into the current, into a riffle where a trout might rise.

In the morning, he took his father's fly rod off the rack and walked again to the riverbank. He laid a cast downstream, and in the same bend where the ashes had disappeared, hooked a keeper brook trout.

He fried the fish whole to accompany bacon and two eggs over easy for breakfast. Samuel straightened his father's bed where he had slept. He washed the dishes, swept the cabin floor, and took a last look around before locking the door.

He guided the Dodge slowly through the forested two track that led to the main gravel road. Just across the entrance bridge, he watched a motherly ruffed grouse showing her brood how to aid digestion by chewing on pebbles, like a cow chews a cud.

Samuel smiled to himself at the thought of the clay urn riding shotgun. His father would appreciate that.

Waiting

"March. I like to prune in March," Papa Firestone always reminded him. "By May the sap will run."

Samuel lay spread-eagle on the orchard grass and felt the spring sun warm his face. Family, soon his family would arrive at the cabin. Angelique and Marie planned to leave St. Simons at noon, the letter advised, the moment Dougal's preschool let out for the summer. All had been packed, ready for departure.

Dougal, his son, attended nursery school at the Old Stone Episcopal Church on the Island. Samuel remembered the night on the bank of the St. Croix River, their last night together. He still felt the merging, as he had every night and every day since.

How is it possible to feel something so powerful only in your mind?

Samuel sat up and tied the laces on his work boots. He pulled the bone handled knife from the sheath, cut short lengths from leftover baling twine, and stuffed them in the left pocket of his work vest. He had sharpened Firestone's pruning shears the way his father taught him. A dull cut might kill a vine.

The fieldstone fire pit began to fill with red cuttings. Firestone had left his son some work, as if his father knew he would never finish.

Samuel pruned each plant, completing the unique sculptures his father had begun. He worked slowly. He wanted to save a few vines to teach Dougal the art of pruning.

THE WAY NORTH

Marie had lain in bed and listened to the relaxing sound of ocean waves lapping near the shore. Something troubled her thoughts. She had seen a red-tailed hawk the previous evening, one of Firestone's favorite birds but not often seen on the island. The clanging telephone startled her, and she jumped from the bed to answer.

A cardinal perched on the tulip tree outside the kitchen window.

After the initial shock, the whole Island buzzed with excitement. Down at the Co-op, Old Marge spared no one the story.

"Nearly a miracle," she exclaimed. "We've lost Firestone, our Rock, but Samuel has come back home."

Marie packed the picnic basket while Angelique picked up Dougal from the church school. She had baked cinnamon rolls, carefully cut them into a manageable size, and wrapped them individually in aluminum foil. Of course, she took a moment for herself on the porch to taste just one. The white, creamy glaze warmed her insides. She rocked and sipped her coffee.

She wouldn't make the trip north.

My place is here, in the islands.

Marie would remember Firestone here and keep the cottage in good order for the kids, as Hector always had.

My family will return, with the seasons, and I will be here to make them a home.

Sheriff Callaghan pulled up in the drive with Ellie alongside. Marie smiled at the unlikely pair and gave Ellie a big hug. She released all the bad thoughts she may have harbored, *let them be forgotten and blown away with the breeze,* as Firestone would have advised.

Right behind them, Emily parked her little Corvair sedan. Old Marge struggled to get out, "Damn, they sure don't make cars like they used to."

Friends who had become family, each and every one, had a part in raising the children, They had come to see Dougal and Angelique off for their trip to Northern Michigan.

Yellow Dog announced Dougal's arrival like a trumpeter proclaiming the king. As always, Angelique let him out at the end of the drive. Dougal followed the dog, trying his best to keep up. Yellow Dog turned several times to check on the boy. Unquestionably, Yellow Dog watched over Dougal.

Angelique left the Volvo door open and called out, "Hey Mama, just let me freshen up, and we'll be on our way."

Firestone had insisted on the Volvo the moment Dougal was born. "I'll be damned if a flimsy car will carry my grandson."

Dougal jumped into Marie's waiting arms.

Though somewhat disappointed with her mother's decision to wait, Angelique understood. Truth be known, she anxiously looked forward to having some time alone with Samuel and their son.

Dougal watched from the car window and questioned everything he saw. He noticed the change in landscape from the salt flats of seacoast Georgia to the palms of South Carolina. He made Angelique pull the car over so he could watch a wild pig scurry into the sawgrass. A great Blue Heron launched deliberately, disturbed by the commotion.

Angelique stopped before dark at a roadside motor lodge in the mountains of western Virginia. After bringing in their bags, she took Dougal and Yellow Dog on a hike up into the hills behind the lodge. The melodious tones of a mountain bluebird carried them up the trail, until they finally spotted the source of the music.

Yellow Dog playfully chased a black squirrel up an oak tree.

They sat on a rock outcropping with an overview of the valley before them. Strangely quiet, Dougal seemed to understand his mother's thoughts. So much time had passed, yet she knew Samuel would embrace her as if nothing had happened. Angelique could only imagine the joy Samuel would take in the first sight of his son. She held the boy's hand while they watched the first stars emerge in the heavens.

Yellow Dog led the pair back down the mountain in the dark. Dougal had no fear of the shadows created by trees that blocked the moon's glow.

"Tomorrow," Angelique held Dougal's face in her hand, "tomorrow you will meet your father."

GRAPEVINES

Arms flailing, eyes smiling, Dougal leapt from the old, square Volvo before his mother unbuckled her seatbelt. The towheaded boy ran to Samuel without pause. Yellow Dog climbed over Angelique to get out and sprinted to catch up. The dog read the happy vibrations in the air and clearly understood, as if he knew Samuel was Papa's son and Dougal's father.

Samuel dropped the pruning shears and bent his knees. He opened his arms and braced himself for the force of the blow. Chest met chest. Dougal grabbed and squeezed. Samuel caressed the boy and smelled his hair and kissed the top of his head.

Yellow Dog knocked the pair to the ground, and with his tail aflutter, licked Samuel's face.

Angelique watched her boys sprawled on the warm, June grass. The muddy barn cat meowed and stepped out from his hiding spot in the long grass behind the arbor. Muddy looked cautiously at Yellow Dog but trusted Samuel to protect him, and he wanted some attention, too.

Samuel stood, walked down the small rise with Dougal tugging at the cuffs of his jeans.

Angelique closed the car door, and with her eyes down, sauntered toward Samuel.

Samuel reached out and raised her chin, gazed into her sparkling green eyes, and kissed Angelique so deeply they tasted each other's salty tears.

"I am so sorry I left you by the river. I thought it for the best," Angelique sobbed.

Angelique fit snugly beneath his shoulders while they embraced. Time fell away, "No need to talk. Now is all that matters."

Angelique's slender fingers clutched at Samuel's strong shoulders as he reached down to pick up his son, who stared wide-eyed at his father.

"Papa told me you would come home, he told me, Dad."

A Party to Remember

Folks from town began arriving early the next morning. Tommy and Jim, two of Firestone's hunting buddies, drove across the grass on the far side of the house while Samuel and Angelique waved and sipped coffee on the porch. Dougal tried to pet the muddy cat, but Yellow Dog intervened, wanting to play with his new friend.

Tommy began arranging kindling in the fieldstone fire pit, and Jim followed with split sugar maple. Each swung a longneck Old Style in their free hand. Jim lifted an iron roasting spit from the bed of the pickup, and they dug the iron legs into place before lighting the fire. Dougal and Samuel looked on from a safe distance.

As if on cue, an hour later, when the coals began to glow, Don, who owned the IGA market in town, drove up with his son and a cooler in the back end of their Bronco. Tommy skewered the whole, skinned pig with a six-foot iron rod. The four of them in unison set the rod on the spit.

"Watch now, Dougal," Tommy called out to the boy.

They had roasted pigs before.

Jim set a lawn chair on the upwind side of the fire near the crank handle of the spit. Tommy brought over a cooler of iced longnecks. For the next seven hours, they took turns cranking the pork to perfection. A casual observer might think the quantity of beer would spoil the operation, but Tommy and Jim were woodsmen. Folks swore their legs were hollow.

In mid-afternoon, cars began pouring up the long drive. The whole town, it seemed, showed up carrying covered dishes. Angelique strung white party lights from the house to the shed. Norma, who owned the local tavern, set up a makeshift bar on a picnic table. A help-yourself keg of Irish Red sat in the shade of the shed overhang.

When all had gathered round, Dougal brought out the clay urn. He used the red Swiss Army knife his mother had given him to pry open the lid. Samuel carefully lifted seven stones from the cairn that his father had built in the front yard. The balanced stone monument, when viewed in line with another cairn a hundred yards or so down the drive, marked magnetic north and south. Firestone had always wanted to know exactly where he stood in the world.

Dougal reached in for a small handful of dust; Samuel a bit more. Together they tossed the ashes into the cairn. A kilted Canadian friend of Firestone's stepped forward and played "Amazing Grace" on the pipes.

A red-tailed hawk soared above the fray.

Stone by many colored stone, Samuel showed Dougal how to read their weight and shape.

"Balance is the key," he explained to his son, as his father had explained to him. When they finished, of course, the cairn looked different than when they started.

Stones can never be replaced in exactly the same way.

The McCarty brothers set up their instruments and amplifier on the back deck. Some others brought out guitars and joined in for folk rock and bluegrass. Samuel brought out the Martin, and with Dougal at his feet and Angelique rubbing his shoulders, picked solos on his well-practiced favorites. Dancing and singing, even those who could neither dance nor sing, lifted the communal spirit.

And when Angelique danced, everyone watched.

"A party to remember," Samuel said softly to himself, knowing that Firestone smiled down from above.

In the Morning

Dougal jumped up on the queen bed, unable to wait until his mom and dad woke up. In the midst of the celebration, he had fallen asleep in a lawn chair with Yellow Dog watching over him. He climbed over Samuel and snuggled between them under flannel sheets.

Firestone's friends had cleaned up the yard before leaving, so after coffee and French-Canadian pancakes, Samuel and his son headed to the grape arbor. Dougal learned quickly, as his father had. He cut sharply on the diagonal, and within the hour, began suggesting where the next cut might be made.

"How about here, Dad?"

Angelique gathered up and washed several casserole dishes. She loaded them into the Dodge, and she and Yellow Dog made a run to town. She wanted to thank the ladies, and she wanted Dougal to have some time alone with his father.

The boy grew bored after a while, just as Samuel had. Though smart as a whip, Dougal was still a little boy. Samuel filled a skin with fresh water from the well and suggested a walk around their land.

A bald eagle perched on the aspen that hung on a steep angle over the upper pasture. The bird seemed to know when the dog was gone, and the man and boy gave him no need to worry. From the high branches, the eagle scanned their twenty-acre alfalfa field that grew a lush green. Purple flowers accented the hay grasses and helped to shield mice and rabbits from the predator's search.

Father and son walked the high field borders. Samuel pointed out where the property lines ran. There were no fences. Neighbors, country folk all, respected the land and each other's privacy.

The pair walked the grade down toward the creek. Samuel had brought his ultra-light rod and showed Dougal how to take the first cast. A tiny brook trout hit. Dougal admired the shimmering color of the fish and watched as his father gently returned the creature to the stream.

"The fridge is full of leftover pulled pork. We'll let that fish grow; maybe catch him again next year."

Near the top of the grade, Dougal, growing tired from the walk, asked to sit on a boulder and rest.

"You know your way back, right son? Just fifty yards up the trail. I'll meet you at the grape arbor."

From the height of the stone, Dougal could see the whole ravine through the light green growth of popple leaves. In the gaps between the trunks of red pine, he saw the creek where he had caught his first brook trout. He was anxious to tell his mother about the fish.

A few feet away, a partridge flushed and disappeared into the treetops. The sound of flapping wings startled the boy until he realized it was a bird.

He watched a speckled fawn clumsily work its way down the far slope to the muddy bottom where the creek narrowed. A mother doe looked on.

Dougal's attention followed a bright red cardinal who perched on a pine branch. His melodious whistle called for a mate.

"Mind if I sit?"

Dougal handed the skin to the old man, never wondering where he had come from.

"Say hello to your father for me. I've missed him."

The fawn had climbed the near slope from the creek and wandered onto the trail. The female cardinal joined the male on the branch.

The movement caused Dougal to turn his head. The pair of birds, one deep red, the other a motherly brown, launched upward toward the cabin where Samuel filled the birdfeeder.

The leather skin lay at Dougal's feet. The boy climbed off the boulder and ran up the trail.

He reached the yard just as Angelique pulled up the drive in the Dodge.

Samuel walked from the cabin. "Dad, Dad, I met an old man down in the woods. He said he missed you."

"I know, Son."

Angelique smiled.

SETTLING IN

After the grapes sweetened, after the juice turned to wine, after the sweetcorn had been blanched and frozen, after the summer houses had been put away for the long winter up north, Samuel took his family west.

Dougal had grown through the summer as fast as the corn. The sun browned his skin; he never burned. Samuel always gooped up with coconut lotion against the rays, but like his mother, Dougal only became more olive beautiful with their days working the farm.

Mornings after coffee became Samuel's time alone. Angelique would walk with the boy or take a trip to town to shop for supper or read with Dougal quietly on the porch. Samuel spent an hour or two alone with his thoughts and the journal that Libby had given him. He had refilled the pad many times and began to organize his words while sitting and dreaming at his father's old desk in his father's old study. He felt at home with his legacy.

Samuel stared out the study window at a leaf leftover from fall. A breeze played with the brown shape on the ground beneath the bird feeder. He watched for an indeterminate time while the leaf changed into a tiny bird before shifting back into a leaf.

Samuel had also taken on the upkeep of a few of Firestone's cottages on the lake in town. He was not handy like his father, but he knew all the locals and knew whom to call. Folks always answered his calls. He had a way about him. People liked Samuel because he treated them fairly and made sure they received an honest wage for honest work.

The summer swells up for a few weeks from Chicago or St. Louis or Memphis tried to take advantage of some less-savvy locals, but Samuel would have none of it. He knew that an upbringing based on hard work and an understanding of nature meant more than capital letters following a signature or a big bank account. Most of the new cottage dwellers inherited their places and their boats from Daddy or Grandpa and lived on trust income. They fought with their siblings over pieces of the pie. From Firestone, Samuel inherited good sense and the respect of the community. In return he felt a duty toward his friends.

Most afternoons, the family tended the farm together, except when the sun shone too hot, and they piled in the Dodge and drove to the lake for a swim. On particularly warm, humid evenings, when flies hatched, Angelique knowingly waved her men off to the river. Dusk came late, often not until after ten, and a man had to be on the river at just the right time to land a big, brown trout. The river ran swiftly, and Samuel held tightly on to Dougal.

They spent that first summer getting to know each other again. September came along in sunny, fresh glory.

"Our secret," Samuel would say. "The summer folks are gone back to their city lives down south, and the lakes are still warm. Don't tell anyone."

In October, Dougal shot his first partridge with Samuel's old lightweight, single shot .410. Yellow Dog turned out to be a natural retriever. Samuel knocked down another, and Angelique cooked the tender birds stuffed with scallions and wrapped in bacon.

"You are a Thompson, son. And we never kill another being except for food," Samuel advised his son.

"I know, Dad. Papa told me."

They joined hands at the table and sang a short blessing for the abundance they enjoyed.

Dougal came to learn what his father knew to be true: We are what we eat. The occasional ribeye steak became a feast. Fresh salads from the garden, brook trout from the streams, and the plump breasts of a ruffed grouse, like these, provided protein. Angelique learned Marie's talent for baking, so their tummies never went begging.

Dougal pinned the brown and white partridge tail feathers to the wall above his bed. He had taken over his father's attic room. Angelique and Samuel moved into the master suite. She converted her sleeping porch into a sort of sitting room, where she closed her eyes and remembered her nights watching for the light in Samuel's window. On rainy mornings, they took their coffee there while Dougal munched on granola.

On such a morning, Angelique recalled their trip with Firestone to Hector's wake. She recanted the tales of their father, how he first went west, how he met Sally on Bear Butte. As he rubbed the clay urn, Samuel's eyes watered. He recalled his own trip to the sacred mountain and realized Angelique had never been there. Samuel missed his father and regretted never seeing the way Firestone looked at Dougal. He seldom spoke aloud but wrote down his feelings in his journal.

Samuel set to winterizing the cabin in early November. Deer season would be starting soon, and he wanted to take his family away before the crazies from downstate started shooting. Dougal would be finishing kindergarten at the private school on St. Simons after Christmas. Angelique had begun to show.

Before returning south to Marie and the cottage on the barrier islands, Samuel was drawn to travel west with a clay pot containing his father's ashes.

CHAPTER FIFTEEN:
1974

Return to the Good Mountain

Snow spit with the wind and left tiny, round, white balls on the Volvo's windshield. Coming across Minnesota and the vast empty two-lane highways of South Dakota, they had avoided major winter storms. The sun had come out briefly when they stopped to admire the monument to Sitting Bull outside of Mobridge, South Dakota. A statue of the iconic Native American looks south over the broad Missouri River valley. The grounds were unkempt, with trash strewn about and barrier fences falling from a lack of maintenance. Even Yellow Dog seemed to frown.

As they drove on west, Samuel recounted his fortunate meeting with Libby at the Custer National Battlefield, known to the Cheyenne as Greasy Grass.

"Another example," Samuel looked at Angelique and their son, "A lack of respect, a mistreatment of history."

Along the gravel road beneath Bear Butte, winter caught the Thompson family. Angelique made sure that Dougal had buttoned his coat and pulled the stocking cap over his ears. Samuel reached into the pot and brought out about half of the remaining grey dust, which he bundled into a torn piece of Firestone's favorite flannel shirt.

Like climbing a natural spiral staircase, they battled the wind and pushed forward. Dougal spotted a red tail hawk soaring high above them in the currents.

"Look, Dad, maybe that's Papa Firestone."

Samuel smiled. "His spirit will always watch over us, Son."

A few hundred yards from the peak of the Good Mountain, years of wind erosion had etched out a small plateau. Standing there, they looked out in all four directions. Spoken words were unnecessary, even for the boy. The sun shone for a moment and lightened the landscape. The white-tinged browns of the stony mountain, the last faded green leaves of the wild grapevines that grew along the trail, and the vivid blue of the prairie lake water all came to life. The hawk leapt from his perch on the peak and rode the wind. A few buffalo grazed on the gentle slopes far below.

Samuel opened the bundled rag of Black Watch plaid, and the northwest wind scattered grains of dust into the southern sky. Clouds rolled in and covered the sun as Firestone's ashes settled into the Black Hills.

"Papa is with Sally again," Angelique whispered.

"He is free," Samuel replied.

The threesome hugged against the cold, and then laughing, bounded down the trail. Samuel tied the shirt fragment to the woody base of a wild grape vine.

The Volvo kicked over on the first try but took several minutes to warm up. Samuel's voice echoed in a joyful, affected tenor, "St. Simons, here we come."

Chapter Sixteen:
1974

SALT AIR

Angelique pushed off the bow of *Wanderer* and the sleek wooden sail craft took her head with the wind abaft the starboard beam. Dougal squeezed in next to his father on the small cockpit seat. Samuel minded the main sheet, a tug here and a loosening there, with his left hand. In his right, he felt the pull of the tide against the tiller.

Morning sickness and the thought of rocking in rolling green waves kept Angelique ashore.

Samuel tacked to guide the boat out past the St. Simons Sea buoy, then tied off the sheet. He placed Dougal's small hand beneath his own on the tiller. *Wanderer* passed the buoy close aboard where they could hear the clanging of deep, uneven ring tones. Even in the two-foot swells, the buoy bounced like a growling dog on the heavy two-inch chain anchored to the bottom.

Samuel released pressure gradually before he took his hand away and shifted to a padded seat on the port side.

"You've got her, Son. Balance the tiller while making sure the wind fills the main sail. Steer due east, to the Gulfstream, zero-nine-zero on the compass."

Four pelicans glided along with the boat, like jet fighters in formation ready to protect an aircraft carrier from attack. A pair of dolphins played in the bow wake. Dougal had the knack; someday *Wanderer* would be his.

After an hour or so, for time passes unnoticed in the wind, the ocean flattened out in the center of a minor front.

"Release the sheet while I let down the main."

Bubbles floated by in a northerly pattern, and soon the boat followed. They had reached the Gulfstream.

Samuel held Dougal by the legs, "Touch the ocean, Dougal Dee. Feel the warmth."

"Your Grandfather Firestone brought me here when I was your age. Papa said that we could ride this warm ocean river all the way home to Scotland."

Samuel felt the clay urn one last time before passing it to his son. Dougal rubbed the smooth curved sides of the pot for a moment before meeting his father's eyes. The boy dropped the urn into the sea.

# EPILOGUE

Spring Break, 1978

Several years have passed, and within the years, seasons. Some vintages tasted better than others, but each holiday, the Thompson family and their lifelong friends uncork a bottle or two, and drink to gentle spirits, both present and passed on.

Everyone has come. After a hearty breakfast, they catch the ferry to Cumberland Island.

Libby and Alexandra made the long trek south from the border-lands. Dougal, who has grown tall and strong, plods ahead on the beach to keep up with Yellow Dog, who watches over Sally Jane just as he watched over Dougal only a short time ago. Samuel never gave the dog another name.

Samuel and Angelique walk hand in hand, following the crowd, following the children. The white mansion burned last year. Only the stone hearth and chimney remain. The property has reverted to the public domain. Ponies munch on grass growing among the rubble.

Marie, sprite and lively despite her greying hair, hurries while remembering the ponies that first morning. Josie has made the trip from Texas. Ellie and Old Marge each hold an arm, like bookends, around Sheriff Callaghan.

Marie points out the spot where she first came ashore.

The family comes together near a dune to sit in the sand and consider the green ocean. Porpoise dive in the shallows. The ponies are curious. Yellow Dog barks at the break of an incoming wave.

Sally Jane runs splashing through the surf.

Her big brother chases in jest.

About the Author

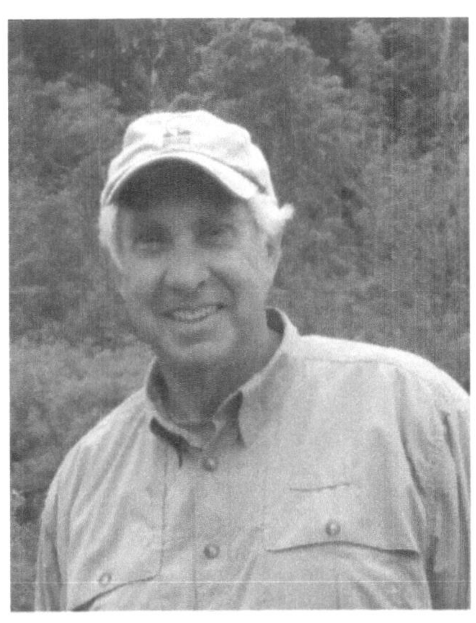

Tom Conlan lives, writes, and tends his modest grape vines on a small farm in the highlands of Northern Michigan. He has captained a Coast Guard Cutter, sailed the world's lakes and oceans, and now searches for the elusive brook trout in backwater streams.

Tom's prose and poetry has appeared in numerous literary journals, as well as *Michigan Trout Magazine*. His lyrical memoir *My Journey Begins Where the Road Ends...* was released in June 2017.

He is currently working on a visual, poetry collection entitled, *Secret Conversations*.

Tom attended the Iowa Writer's Workshop, holds a Master of Fine Arts in Creative Writing from Queens University of Charlotte and a Master of Science from the US Naval Postgraduate School in Monterey, California. Learn more about Tom on his website at www.thomasfordconlan.com.